IT'S ALL THE
BANKS' FAULT

STAATS JES RAU

M

IT'S ALL THE BANKS' FAULT

WHAT IT TAKES TO STOP
THE DESTRUCTIVE FORCE
OF THE BANKS AND
SAVE THE ECONOMY

Library of Congress Control Number: 2012912142
ISBN: Hardcover   978-1-4771-3897-7
               Softcover   978-1-4771-3896-0
               Ebook   978-1-4771-3898-4

To order additional copies of this book, contact:
Xlibris Corporation
1-888-795-4274
www.Xlibris.com
Orders@Xlibris.com
114902

Contents

Everybody knows by now that the banks have tremendous power. The true nature of their power—and their weakness—reveals itself only by a long term analysis.

Twenty years ago, Jes Rau came to the conclusion that the economy goes through Long Waves, as the Russian economist Nikolai Kondratieff had discovered almost a century ago. Kondratieff had no explanation for the curves which the compiled data of output and prices showed.

Jes Rau on the other hand starts out with a theory of the Long Wave. For him the instability of the long term economic development is a built-in quality of our current monetary system. The flaws of Central Bank money become apparent as Rau explains the misconceptions of the mainstream monetary theory which shapes the economic thinking of the politicians and the public at large. This book will set all of us free from bad thinking which leads to terrible results. This book can change the world. It's all a matter of the mind.

Twenty years ago Jes Rau predicted that at the turn of the century the world economy would approach the abyss of a depression. He was right on target. His prediction was based on pure logic.

If the politicians understand the logic they will be able to overcome the current crisis and choose a policy mix which permits continuing economic growth without any inflation. Above all, people must discard their belief in the stork who drops the newborne money out of thin air on the banks. Jes Rau advocates adopting money which "behaves" like gold. By empowering the Mint as the regulator and distributor of money it is possible to avoid the depression and to overcome the pull of the Long Wave. By empowering the Mint the U.S. budget deficits lose their menace and those who predict gloom and doom and the decline of America because of it's "debt" will be recognized as false prophets.

The economist Jes Rau is the publisher of two German-American newspapers, the New York Staats-Zeitung and the California Staats-Zeitung. He lives with his wife Margita and their four children Marlene, Maximilian, Juliane and Jes in Sarasota, Florida

Preface

"It's all the bank's fault." Truer words were never spoken, you may think. But please, don't expect me to tell juicy stories about the boundless greed of the bankers and about their misuse of their exceptional powers. Of course, such stories must be told because they highlight the urgent need for reform. But I am not the right guy to do so. I know that greed exists. Actually, we all experience it every day. Nothing new under the sun.

But this book is not about the perceived character flaws of some moneylenders. It is about the flaw of the existing monetary system, which burdens the banks with responsibilities they are not equipped to handle. Banks are supposed to be the best allocators of resources because supposedly they are channeling credit to its most productive use. There is truth in that notion, but only some truth. From a certain stage on, the banks have no other choice than funding projects which are profitable to them, but highly destructive to the economy.

This concept is the foundation on which my "general theory" of *Die Welle* ("the wave") rests, which allowed me twenty years ago to predict that at the turn of the century, the

American economy would reach the stage of the Depression—if the government wouldn't take decisive countermeasures. Twenty years is a long time in our lives. Even a Mercedes needs some repairs after two decades. But there are some things which get more valuable with age. This product of my imagination is one of them, I think. It may be outdated as its predictions have already come true. But the accuracy of the predictions gives an almost-eerie credibility to the logic they are based on.

"He who forgets the past is doomed to repeat it." I love this quote, which is attributed to the Spanish-American philosopher George Santayana. For this purpose, I would like to tailor it more to the needs of the economist that I am and rephrase it: he who doesn't understand the past economic development cannot understand the current economic development and is doomed to repeat the past.

You may be familiar with John Maynard Keynes's quip: "In the long run we are all dead." By this, Keynes expressed his disregard for those economists who tried to extract knowledge from discerning the past. Here the great master erred. Actually, he was dead wrong, I think. Only a long-term analysis provides us the insights necessary to understand our current situation and to lay the groundwork for a bright future for all of us.

Many thoughts which entered this book I have carried with me over a long time. Already as a student at Tübingen, the German university town, I nurtured some doubt on whether the banks should have the responsibility for regulating the money supply. When I started working in New York as the business correspondent of a German newspaper, I came to the conclusion that almost everything which could be read in the press about the "evil deficits" of the U.S. federal government was totally wrong. After all, why did Jimmy Carter fail, while Ronald Reagan succeeded? Jimmy Carter, the moralist, kept tight control of the finances, while Ronald Reagan let the budget deficit soar. Was there some lesson to learn?

Well, newspaper editors prefer to play it safe. Political correctness reigns. If the facts do not match the prevailing strain of thoughts, they are overlooked. Who dares to think differently risks being silenced, fired, and treated like an outcast. Of course, that is the risk every truly free thinker faces. This is not a complaint—not at all. We are talking here actually about the essence of a free society: It doesn't permit heretic thinkers to be burnt anymore like in the good old days. It silences them by more peaceful means. That's quite an improvement, I would say. How else can a society deal with its "crackpots"? It's up to those to prove the majority wrong. And that's what I am trying to do by publishing this book.

Oh, am I grateful, that even a former German chancellor doesn't have the power to send a rebellious economist to a gulag in Siberia. I was spared this fate of Nikolai Kondratieff, who dared to contradict Stalin.

I dedicate this work to my hero, Nikolai Kondratieff, who was an outstanding economic thinker and a very brave man. His concept of the long wave inspired me to find its cause and, by doing so, to formulate the "General Theory of economic development," which Keynes attempted to write. Keynes failed splendidly, I may say. I admire Keynes very much. He is undoubtedly the greatest economist of all times. And I have no ideological bones to pick with today's Keynesian economic thinkers like Paul Krugman.

The difference is that I consider the Keynesian theory incomplete—its disregard for the long-term view is only one of its shortcomings. Because of these shortcomings, the Keynesian remedies are often ineffective and may even have disastrous consequences.

When I became a journalist, I accepted the role journalists are playing in our society. They are not the real opinion makers—they are mostly just amplifiers of rivaling ideologies and concepts. Most journalists do not offer their own deep thoughts—they ask questions and let the experts give the answers. A successful journalist picks the creed which fits him best—conservative or liberal, for example—and then follows its lead. A journalist is a person with modest aspirations. He is not a genuine thinker, but an intermediate—a middleman. Like bankers, journalists don't own most of the wares they are distributing. They get the stuff from somebody else.

In 1987 I realized that I was unfit to play this role of a journalist. I discovered that I was a thinker, not an opinion salesman. Tracking the economic development, I had come to the conclusion that a crash of the stock market was imminent. The untold story is that the German Bundesbank had pressured then—Fed chairman Alan Greenspan to raise interest rates with the purpose of reigning in the trade deficit of the USA. I grasped immediately what this would mean for the stock market. But my article predicting the crash was never printed—the only one I ever wrote, which ended up in the trash I was told that the publisher, a former German chancellor, no less, had intervened because he felt I was mixing up money and credit.

When the crash occurred on that Monday, October 19 (I had even picked the right day), I felt cheated. Please, excuse my vanity. But I thought I had deserved the fifteen minutes of worldwide fame which everybody is entitled to, according to Andy Warhol. I consoled myself with the thought that I now surely had earned some respect for my way of thinking. But being right is obviously an insult to some people. The campaign against me continued. The editor in chief, who got his education at the school for the Nazi elite, knew how to get rid of this contrarian.

Never in my life will I forget how my colleagues at a conference of the newspaper treated me like a living dead—they looked right through me, as if they did not know me. I was paralyzed by shame—shame for my fellow journalists of the supposedly liberal newspaper which I loved. And I felt shame (and some sort of pity) for the man whom I had considered my best friend and who had betrayed me to advance his own career. He lived happy ever after. Treason is worth it, it seems.

Well, sometimes a personal disaster proves to be a blessing in disguise. I decided to feel grateful for those who engineered this sudden turn in my life. For one, I got rid of the illusion that any established newspaper could serve me as a platform for thoughts which contradict the general consensus. Questioning the evilness of budget deficits of the federal government is like questioning motherhood and apple pie. You can do that only at your own peril. So consider yourself duly warned about the content of this book. It may put you at odds with your mother-in-law and most other red-blooded people.

But you may learn some fundamental truths about the working of the capitalist system within the framework of central bank money.

For me, the crash of 1987 was above all the confirmation that I was on the right track with my economic thinking. After my involuntary departure from *Die Zeit* in spring 1988, I frantically began to write down the ideas which I had planned to submit to that newspaper for publication. The first three chapters were quickly written because I had them already formulated in my head. The following chapters were more difficult. It was my fear that I would never be able to finish it when on September 1, 1989, I took over the *New Yorker Staats-Zeitung* and was suddenly involved in a struggle to save the oldest German-language newspaper in America. This change from the role of a reporter to the role of a publisher was not easy for me. Being a businessman had never been a goal of mine. But I considered all the headaches of running a business a fair price for being able to write freely and unafraid of censorship. Unfortunately, I had very little time left to work on the theory of long-term economic development.

At the beginning of 1990 the work was finally done.

Having completed the task I had set myself, all my ambitions were exhausted. I had more pressing matters to take care of than going through the motions of publishing a book, which was probably destined to encounter either indifference or hostility. The manuscript was collecting dust in a drawer.

I don't know where all the years have gone. But suddenly the year 2000 wasn't a date in a science fiction novel anymore. The turn of the century had arrived. I had stopped keeping track of the long waves. But suddenly I noticed, to my own surprise, that the economy had actually reached the stage when the dreaded Depression was looming—as I had predicted.

In the issue for August 31, 2002, the *New Yorker Staats-Zeitung* appeared with the picture of a big wave with the wording "Riding the Big Wave—into the Depression." The world stood at the abyss to the Depression, but nobody seemed to notice. On the title page of the *Staats* I wrote pleadingly, "Please, listen to me."

In the following issues of our newspaper, we published most of the manuscript in installments. In order to bring the text up-to-date, I made some corrections of the original manuscript and I added a few sentences. But I refrained from rewriting it. I am thankful to the readers of the *New Yorker Staats-Zeitung* for digesting this difficult text without complaint. The very positive reaction of some readers was encouraging.

The text of the German-language version of this book (*Die Banken sind an Allem Schuld*) is mostly identical to the text stored in computer files which I used for the publication in the *Staats* newspaper. The readers therefore have to cope with a few inconsistencies. I did not try to repair these blemishes. So you will still be treated with predictions for the turn of the century although this time had long passed. And I stick with the "prediction" that in 2000 the American economy would reach the tipping point to the Depression. In my view, two external factors postponed the onset of the Depression: the Bush tax cut and the policy of re-inflating the economy pursued by the Federal Reserve Bank under the leadership of Alan Greenspan. These measures could not have a lasting effect, especially after the Federal Reserve changed its course when Ben Bernanke took charge.

What happened next fits pretty much into my concept of the long waves. I didn't know anything about subprime loans and about the securitization of mortgage loans when I wrote this book. But these are details which are not important for the formulation of a theory. These banking tricks are just another form of the demonetization of money, which has taken place over centuries.

I have asked myself whether it would make sense to publish this treatise in the form of a book. I am eager to finally switch my attention to other matters. But I concluded that the message included in describing the path of the long waves is important and worth spreading. I hope enough people will study the text and will understand its ramifications for almost everybody.

Some friends and readers have urged me to get the manuscript translated into English. Only then it would reach its potential, they argued. I agreed, but finding a translator who could help me proved to be impossible. Translating is a difficult job. I could not do it myself. Therefore I decided to narrate the content in English, meaning, I didn't bother to translate each sentence verbatim but I told the story anew—only in English. I don't know if I will get all the bugs out of the text and make it run smoothly. I hope the result is good enough to make the readers understand that by discarding some entrenched myths—like the myth of the *Klapperstorch* who drops the newborn money on the banks—new possibilities become apparent, new methods to stabilize the economy are possible.

I am convinced that the current crisis can be overcome if today's central bank money is replaced by money which "behaves" like gold. mint money, that is.

I hope that after studying the following ten chapters you will understand what I am talking about and will agree that the course of action I propose is the right one. If enough of you come to this conclusion, this thin volume may result in a big improvement in the monetary policy of this great country, making the dollar as good as gold, letting the economy grow without inflation, and thus improve the life of many, many human beings.

Chapter 1
Rediscovering the Long Wave

The twenty-first century promises to become the era of global capitalism. This is not a very original thought, I admit. After all, there seems to be no alternative to capitalism left after the Communist bloc collapsed. The paradise on earth which Marx, Lenin, Stalin, and Mao promised to the proletarians proved to be a rather unattractive destination.

By now even dyed-in-the-wool socialists must admit that most people prefer to be exploited by "greedy capitalists" (or to join the exploiters) than to suffer the egalitarian shortages and the miserable quality of the products and services typical for an economic system which promises to fulfill the collective needs and aspirations instead of the desires of the selfish individual.

The plenty of products and services, the wealth of many people, and the high living standards of the population, which the market economy is able to provide, is truly amazing. The pace of the technical and economic change, generated by the never-ending chase for profits within the framework of a market economy ruled by competition, is mind-boggling. The same word comes to mind as we observe the transformation of the national economies into integral parts of the global market.

The eighties and nineties were shaped by the increasing globalization of purchases and sales, which spread the blessings of capitalism from the established industrial countries to other nations. As these countries are integrated into the global economy, they can taste a slice of the global prosperity. Even Russia and China have become part of the worldwide net of capitalism and will become lucrative markets for producers.

The interweaving of the national economies will have the result that one day all people on earth will enjoy the fundamental "rights" the Americans have: a house in the suburb, a chicken in the pot, a computer on the desk, at least one car in the garage, and vacations in Disneyland.

Even the most sour-faced pessimist must admit that the twenty-first century is full of promise and that there are many good reasons to rhapsodize about the magnificent economic future of mankind. But it should not be forgotten that the capitalistic system fundamentally has not changed, even if it may have softened the raw edges over the years. One thing is still the same: capitalism in its current form still harbors the destructive tendencies which triggered the worldwide Depression in the thirties und provided the breeding ground for fascism and communism.

The current economic upswing which began in the early eighties confirms my conviction that we are heading toward a crisis, which will shake the foundations of the world economy as much as the crash and the following Depression sixty years ago. I say this for several reasons. The first one is that the long-lasting boom we are experiencing right now and which will last until the end of the twentieth century fits exactly into the pattern of the long-term economic development which I have detected.

Secondly, this crisis will impact a generation which has only experienced prosperity. Therefore, neither the politicians nor the population will be prepared for the "hurricane."

Thirdly, the obviously "unending" upswing is diminishing the incentive to explore our current economic system further and to develop the tools to deal with its instability.

Isn't it amazing that most economists and politicians don't have a convincing explanation for the length of the current uninterrupted upswing?

Only a few economists and historians have dealt with the topic of the long waves of the economic development. Their existence or nonexistence has become more a matter of faith than rational reasoning. Today, the believers are mostly eccentrics, who are not taken seriously.

While the occupation with shorter business cycles has become a reputable branch of the economic departments of universities, anybody who talks about long-term cycles has as much credibility as astrologers, who are casting horoscopes, predicting our future.

The skeptical attitude is quite understandable because the evidence, offered by those who believe having detected the traces of long economic cycles in history, is very weak. The historic approach is problematic since it depends on historical writing, which rarely deals thoroughly with economic conditions and has no precise economic data to rely on. Yes, the Bible lets us know that God told the Pharaoh by his dreams that Egypt will enjoy seven fat years, which are followed by seven lean years. So we have it from a good authority that a business cycle existed long time ago. But even strong believers in biblical truth will doubt that the Pharaoh's dreams can be used as proof that the concept of a long wave is still relevant today.

The fuzziness of the findings which the "historical school" of economics can offer led John Maynard Keynes to make his famous quip: "In the long run we are all dead."

This is, I may say, another Keynesian truism, which states the obvious truth but is misleading because of its assumption

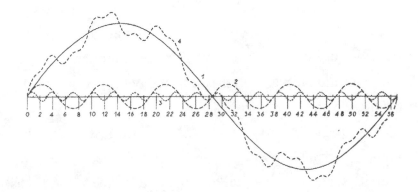

Diagram 1: In his book *Konjunkturtheorien* Schumpeter uses a continuing sinus and cosinus curve to describe Kondratieff's long wave.

that an examination of the long-term development of the economy doesn't help us understand the current situation. I hope I will be able to show that **without an analysis of the forces, which shape the long-term development, the current situation cannot be explained.** And future troubles can only be foreseen, and counteractive measures can only be taken at the right time, if we understand what drives the long-term ups and downs of the observed indices. Detecting the traces of the long waves is only the beginning, formulating a convincing theory would be the next step. A true general theory must be based on the long-term view, not withstanding our mortality in the long run.

The first step in this direction was taken by the Russian economist Nikolai Kondratieff, who attempted to prove the existence of long waves by statistical analysis. Between 1922 and 1928 Kondratieff published several studies which dealt with the long-term business cycle. One of them was translated into German and appeared in the leading economic publication *Archiv für Sozialwissenschaft und Sozialpolitik*. The people who studied this work must have recognized shortly after that this article was the *menetekel*, the writing on the wall, the portent of doom, since one year later the stock market experienced a crash and soon after prices of industrial goods, commodities, and wages dropped, output and incomes contracted—very much like the sequence of data Kondratieff had compiled of earlier depressions.

The only comfort Kondratieff's long wave provided was the notion that at one point in time the economies started to pull out of the depression, paving the way to another phase of expansion.

The latter prediction didn't sit well with Stalin, who considered capitalism doomed forever. Because of his serious aberration from the party line of the Bolsheviks, Kondratieff was sent to a Siberian work camp, where, according to Alexandr Solzhenitsyn, he lost his sanity and died.

In the treatise, translated into German, Kondratieff used rows of data of British, French, and American sources: indices of commodities in relation to the price of gold, quotations of British debt instruments (consols), quotations of French annuities, wages in the British textile industry, wages in the British agriculture, value of British and French foreign trade, coal production in England, consumption of mineral oil in France, production of iron in England, production of lead in England, deposits in accounts at French savings banks, quantity of gold in circulation.

The similarities of the curves, which appear after the data are recorded in a time diagram, become apparent at the first glance. After the application of a complex formula in order to purify the streams of data, the similarities of the curves become even stronger. Kondratieff may or may not have assumed that the curves are more or less synchronic. But on this assumption the curves are based on which Joseph Schumpeter created in order to characterize Kondratieff's long wave. Schumpeter consolidated prices, wages, interest rates as well as indices of production and consumption into **one** curve. To me, that makes as much sense as adding up apples, pears, oranges, and eggs. For that reason Schumpeter's sinus-shaped long wave provides no clue on what the curve is measuring.

I guess when Schumpeter designed this consolidated curve, he did so in order to express the essence of the long wave and to put it in relation to shorter cycles in motion at the same time.

Schumpeter's curve of the long wave is easy to remember, and it seems to make it easy to understand the matter. Unfortunately, this approach is very misleading. I think Schumpeter himself was fooled by his own design of the curve.

After all, any theory based on Schumpeter's Kondratieff curve must come to the conclusion that economic growth is inextricably tied to rising prices and rising interest, while a slowdown of economic activity is tied to a lowering of inflation and interest rates. Schumpeter's Kondratieff wave therefore can be interpreted as a confirmation of the Phillips curve, which is based on Keynesian thinking. But isn't it a historical fact that there were periods when the economy grew without inflation?

This contradiction with historical facts alone proves that Schumpeter's consolidated curve is of little use to understand the forces which create the long waves. I don't want to question the statistics Kondratieff used and his method of whipping them into the shape he needed. But any selection of statistical data and the choice of tricks to turn the data in a recognizable curve are influenced by the intentions of the statistician.

Kondratieff's intention was to distill the similarity of the rows of data he examined. Whether the emerging curves where synchronous or more or less out of phase probably didn't concern him very much.

My approach is completely different. I don't start with any statistics. I have made up an *a priori* theory of the long-term economic development, and I offer you the hypothesis that several rows of indices, which provide significant information on the status of an economy, will have patterns similar to those which Kondratieff's curves revealed. Please have a look at Diagram 2 at the end of this chapter. Each of the four curves have different peaks and different lows but the same turning points. The differences of these curves and their relationship to each other provide the key to the understanding of the long-term cycle.

All four curves seem to have a similar shape if they were rounded. Without a theory you must be inclined to think that divergences are only random variations of the typical pattern.

But I start with a theory. The curves in Diagram 2 are expressions of this theory, meaning that they are just hypothetical in nature. I will leave it to others to compare the curves with historical data. If the statistical data of certain periods do not fit into the pattern shown here, it doesn't mean that my theory is wrong because my curves are only *idealtypisch*—ideals which may be hard to discern in the statistical mirror of reality.

But I am confident that the relevant statistical data of the American and the German economy since the nineteenth century are roughly following these lines. In other cases—like Great Britain—the statistical data may not follow the pattern of my curves because of overriding special influences, like the chronic overvaluation of the pound and because of confiscatory taxation.

You may wonder why one line in the diagram is rounded while the other three are not. For aesthetic reasons I had intended to make the other lines look like deformed sinus curves as well. But then I decided against it because it seemed more important to make the turning point easy to recognize.

So only the curve reflecting the prices of goods and services and the changes in interest rates looks like the curve which Schumpeter had in mind. If you want to, you may consider the curve as *pars pro toto*—the symbol of the long wave. Although long-term economic development cannot be represented by only one curve, I often refer to the long wave in reference for Kondratieff and Schumpeter. But in my opinion at least four curves are needed to characterize the different stages of the long-term economic development:

1. The wave of prices and interest rates

This curve is a consolidation of the development of very different data. Prices of goods and services and interest rates do not always follow the same drummer. But since I do not want to convolute the picture too much, I decided to throw apples and pears into one pot. The rationale behind this is the theory that there is a strong causal relationship between prices and interest rates. Of course, you cannot predict how the central bank reacts to an uptick of inflation. But it is a reasonable assumption that ultimately the central bank will have to increase interest rates to rein in inflation. On the other hand, the central bank will ultimately lower interest rates when inflation rates begin to slide.

There may be a time lag, of course. Such a time lag is typical for inflationary phases when the central bank adjusts interest rates after a long delay to the level of inflation. In an analysis of long-term trends, these lags can be overlooked. At one point of the long waves the consolidation must be given up since interest rates and prices don't go in lockstep anymore.

When I speak of interest rates, I refer to the yields of Treasury bonds and bills, the federal funds rate, the discount rate of the central bank, and the rate on savings, which are all related. The prime rate, the mortgage rates, and other rates for bank loans must at another stage of the long-term development be given special attention because they may diverge substantially from the cost of funds. But to make it less complicated, we consider the changes in the cost of funds as the constituent factors of the first long wave.

2. The wave of economic activity

The second line shows the level of economic activity and production data of various branches. This is our second long wave.

3. The wave of stock prices

The ups and downs of stocks are of course of great interest to everybody who owns some, and there is plenty of literature on the topic how to get rich buying and selling stocks. Most economists though don't give much thought to the role of the stock market and its relationship to the rest of the economy. The stock market is a place for trading assets. The activity of the investors and speculators directly affects the gross national product only, when profits and losses are realized and brokers earn their commission. Since most economists are focused on the determining factors of the national product, to them the stock market seems to be only a sideshow.

Here we are facing one of the structural defects of most economic models, which do not tie the creation of the national product to the fluctuations of the valuation of assets. Considering the huge amounts of money which the stock market soaks up, especially in a bull market, it is surprising that the interaction between the stock market and the rest of the economy has been explored so little.

So therefore, we rely on the common wisdom that rising stock prices are signs of a healthy economy. But the truth is that common sense isn't always right and that the stock market is not always the indicator of economic health. A bull market can be a sign of a severe misdirection of funds. The development of stock prices is our third long wave.

4. The wave of real estate prices

The real estate market is a huge chunk of the economy. Most economists are mostly interested in new construction of homes, which directly affects the national product. But the real estate market has another side: the existing houses, condominiums, and offices are old assets like the stocks.

Since they are made out of real bricks and mortar or wood and plasterboard, houses are considered a safer investment, whose prices are not as volatile as stocks. After all, everybody needs housing. Therefore, the common wisdom is that the real estate market must be more stable. This is a great misconception of the nature of this market, which can be carried away by speculation easily—especially in America, where mortgages are readily available with little down payment.

Like stocks, rising real estate prices are considered a sign or prosperity and are viewed favorably because they provide elder folks a valuable asset when their earning power declines.

But real estate prices are not only a function of the national product, and like stock prices, they are no indicator of economic health.

The prices of stocks and the prices of real estate may move in the same direction most of the time, but the amplitude of the curves can differ substantially. These differences are telltale signs of the state of the economy. Therefore, the real estate prices must be watched carefully, and their fluctuations represent the fourth long wave.

The Four Phases of the Long Waves

The ideal typical long-term economic development goes through different stages, whose character is shaped by the constellation of all four long waves. I have chosen to differentiate four phases. A case can be made to divide the long waves in six segments, but dividing the long waves in four distinctive phases meets our purpose.

1. The first phase of the long waves: recovery and expansion

In the first phase of the long-term cycle, the economy recovers from the preceding depression. An upswing with stable prices is taking place. The curve of prices for goods and services is flat. In the beginning, the upturn of the production is hardly recognizable, but then economic growth gains traction and the gross national product increases rapidly.

In this phase, the economy develops in a perfect fashion. The increasing economic activity leads to full employment. Wages and profits in industry and trade are growing. It seems that all the troubles of yesteryear have disappeared.

The stock market is booming. The real estate market expands as new construction increases the housing stock. Real estate prices are firming, but there is little speculation in old houses. It's the best of all worlds.

2. The second phase of the long waves:
the inflationary upswing

The second phase of the long waves begins with an uptick of the prices of goods and services. At the turning point T11, the inflation is still very low, but it starts to feed itself. After a time lag, interest rates follow the spiral of inflation.

The economy is still growing but slower than before. The turning point T21 marks the beginning of a phase of slower growth of the national product.

The stock market adjusts to the new reality of slower growth and increasing inflation. At the turning point T31, a phase of stagnating stock prices begins. Real estate prices, on the other hand, start to accelerate, beginning at turning point T41. Everybody tries to escape from the devaluation of money by investing in real estate. Soaring prices for land, houses, and condos are typical for this phase of the inflationary upswing.

3. The third phase of the long waves:
the disinflationary upswing

The third phase of the long-term cycle begins at the turning point W12, when the inflationary fever is broken. As soon as the inflation rate is moderating, interest rates follow suit. Now a spiral of lower inflation rates and interest rates is set into motion. The change of the direction of inflation and interest rates affects the whole economy. The national product is growing again, slowly first but gaining speed later on. The stock market is booming. The real estate market languishes for a short time then it goes wild as well. This is the time when huge fortunes can be made by investing in stocks and real estate.

4. The fourth phase of the long waves: the depression

The fourth phase of the long wave announces itself at the turning points T34 and T44, when stock prices and real estate prices collapse.

What comes first, whether the crash of stocks or the collapse of the real estate market, is hard to say. Both markets follow the same drummer, but the depreciation of real estate prices most likely happens at a slower rate and stretches over a longer time.

At this point in time, inflation and the interest rates are approaching the zero percent mark. At the turning point T13, disinflation turns into deflation. The prices for goods and services are going down. Now we have reached the most critical stage of the long waves because at T13 the development of prices and interest rates doesn't follow the same direction

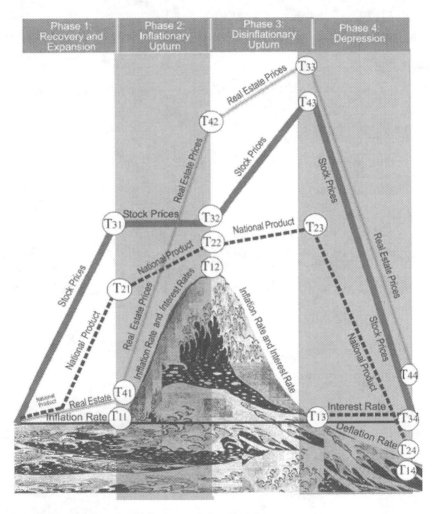

Diagram 2: The four phases of the four long waves

anymore, as interest rates have reached the lowest possible level and can't become negative.

Starting at T23, the production of goods and services is shrinking.

The depression only ends when the national product stops declining. At T34 the prices of stocks suddenly rise, anticipating the beginning of the recovery.

Chapter 2
Schumpeter and Keynes

Now let's embark on the search for the causes of the described long waves. Let's see how far we get applying the methods of Joseph Schumpeter and John Maynard Keynes. Kondratieff himself admitted that he didn't have an explanation for the long waves. In the mentioned article, he only writes that he has the suspicion that the long waves have something to do with *Kapitalakkumulation*. This is a Marxist expression with a dual meaning. At one hand, it means capital investments and the growing amount of real assets due to the investments. On the other hand, *Kapitalakkumulation* means the accumulation of financial assets, the savings.

Now Keynes has taught us that from the bird's-eye view of macroeconomics, total savings always equals total investment. But this is only true if savings is defined as the money spent for investment. But in fact, investments and savings may be related to each other but differ from each other. I am tempted to use the phrase "different as the two sides of a medal." But this may be misleading because contrary to Keynes's belief, savings and investment differ in size.

Schumpeter only took into account one side of the medal, the investment part of *Kapitalakkumulation*. The one-sidedness of his view can be explained by the *Zeitgeist* shaped by the historic circumstances. During the thirties, the political fight was over the fundamental question on capitalism or socialism (or fascist state capitalism). Within the capitalist camp, the economic debate partially raged over the question on which sort of money was the right one for the market economy: gold or central bank money?

Schumpeter's theoretic, historic, and statistic analysis of the capitalistic process, as is the subtitle of his monumental work, explains capitalism in the framework of the central bank monetary system without questioning it.

For Schumpeter, the backbone of the capitalistic system is the entrepreneur. While the socialists see in him mostly the exploiter and parasite, Schumpeter considers the entrepreneur the driving force of the capitalist economy. The "dynamic entrepreneur" plays an almost-heroic role, according to Schumpeter. His drive for profit by making new use of the existing capital assets and his capital investments renews even mature economies and creates employment and prosperity.

From this perspective, Kondratieff's *Kapitalakkumulation* must mean investment, and central bank money must appear to be the only fitting form of money. Because in his view it is the entrepreneur who really has the control over the amount of money created and over its use. Deciding whether to invest or not invest, whether to borrow money or not—the entrepreneur decides about the creation of money.

As central bank money is created by credit issued for the use of the entrepreneur, it is ultimately the debtor who regulates the money supply and directs it to its best use. The central bank and its member banks, according to Schumpeter, only play a more or less passive role. "Whoever attributes to the banks a decisive role in the channeling of the money stream attributes to them a role in the economic process which they don't play," he writes. "By focusing on the amount of credits those economic thinkers completely lose sight of the essential element of purpose. Since it is the debtor, who decides on the purpose of the credit it is he who decides about the direction the flow of funds is taking and not the bank," argues Schumpeter.

In his book *Konjunkturzyklen* he doesn't argue with the proponents of gold money. But his description of the money system based on central bank money sounds very much as a *plaidoyer* against the attacks by the critics who favor a gold-based monetary system.

Schumpeter's passionate support of a monetary system which creates money by issuing credit is founded on the conviction that it serves best the needs of the entrepreneurs. While the amount of money made of gold, silver, or any other valuable metal is limited by the existing supplies of the metals, there is no physical limit for the amount of money created by credit.

Creating central bank money, therefore, is a totally flexible mechanism which in perfect fashion meets the requirement of the entrepreneurs. Finding projects worth financing is the main obstacle which the entrepreneurs are facing. The projects must be lucrative enough to guaranty the payment of interest for the borrowed capital and the repayment of the principal. These conditions for the loans are the only limitations for the supply of new money.

From the central role Schumpeter attributes to the entrepreneur he derives his explanation of the long waves. Their existence is a reflection of the level of success the entrepreneurs are having in finding and realizing new productive investment opportunities which make the economy grow.

The question is then why the investment opportunities change so much over time. Schumpeter's explanation is that the expansive force of innovations and the contractive force of lacking innovations are causing the change of economic activity during the different phases of the long wave.

These innovations can be improvements in production methods or inventions like the steam engine and the railway, the car, and electricity, which the entrepreneur uses to create new products at low prices, which guarantee huge new markets. As the entrepreneurs finance the necessary capital investments by bank loans, they trigger a boom.

When the expansive force of these innovations peters out, the upswing part of the long wave is breaking and the economy begins to go downhill. The slide goes on until the entrepreneurs are coming up with innovations again.

Innovations depend on inventions, which can't be delivered on demand, even if the corporations, the government, and society try to foster a climate which is favorable for inventions. This would mean that a more or less external factor, which is not system immanent, would determine the long wave.

If the statistics show regularity in the sequence of several long waves, as Kondratieff suggests, this would be either by accident or a rhythmic regularity of inventions. The letter is highly implausible. For that reason alone, Schumpeter failed to solve Kondratieff's riddle.

Not one sentence of his huge tome Schumpeter devotes to the possibility to counteract the economic fluctuations in order to avoid the far-reaching effects on the lives of people. Is there no remedy against the sickness of the economy which makes millions of people lose their jobs und suffer great hardship?

The capitalist system, as Schumpeter sees it, obviously offers very few ways to steady the path of economic development. The help which policymakers can provide in Schumpeter's world could only be to give more freedom of action to the entrepreneur and give him a better chance to create new prospering companies out of the ruins and ashes of the bankrupt old corporations. The more innovative the entrepreneurs are, the better are the chances that they can pull the economy out of the doldrums. But only an epochal innovation can really do the trick and create totally new markets and reshape the economy as much as the railways once did and the automobile. Had Schumpeter lived today, he might point to the computer or to the Internet as the driving force of the current long wave.

Schumpeter doesn't deny that the "capitalist process" can be very painful. He even came to the conclusion that mass unemployment, the impoverishment of the middle class, and the collapse of banks and big industrial companies might finish capitalism and lead to one form of socialism or another. He predicted the victory of socialism not because of a socialist conviction. He stuck to capitalism. But he considered himself a realist who understood that the gigantic dislocations, caused by the cyclical nature of capitalism, would shake the foundations of any democracy. He therefore came to the resigned conclusion that the capitalistic system wasn't stable enough to withstand the onslaught of collectivism.

At this point, the thinking of the two giants who still shape the economic thinking goes in different directions. Very much like Schumpeter, John Maynard Keynes considered the businesses and their capital investments as the engine of the economy, and like Schumpeter, Keynes was a proponent of central bank money. For Keynes, gold was the "barbaric metal."

But contrary to Schumpeter, Keynes came to the conclusion that recessions and depressions can be avoided without abandoning the capitalist system.

Keynes thought it was a waste of time to dwell on long-term observations of the economy and formulate theories "for the long run."

He concentrated on analyzing the short-term economic process. For analytical purposes, he used a little system of equations which looked deceptively simple. Over its meaning, some economic thinkers may have almost lost their sanity, I presume (I am one of them).

The system, representing a macroeconomic model of the economy, consists of the following equations:

1. $Y = C = I$ 2. $Y = C = S$
3. $C = I = C = S = I = S$

The first equation says that the gross national product (Y) consists of produced consumer goods and capital investments. The second equation says that the GNP is either spent for consumption (C) or saved (S). Since the gross national product (Y) is identical with the national income (Y), a third equation follows, which says that the expenditures for capital investments amount to the same sum as the money saved.

The thinker of the Classical School thought that the equilibrium of $I = S$ was always put into effect by the mechanism of interest rate changes. If variable interest rates would regulate the level of savings and the level of investments in such a fashion, it would mean that the capitalist system had a built-in thermostat, which would assure the stability of the system.

But the decline of the world economy during the thirties showed that there wasn't such a thermostat. Keynes showed that the economic process worked very differently than believed. Keynes considered saving mostly as nonconsumption. When the reduction of demand by nonconsumption was not filled by the spending for capital investments, the economy must shrink, Keynes concluded.

The level of interest rates (i), according to Keynes, certainly is an important factor in determining the decisions to spend money for capital investments. But the overriding factor is something else. The main question is how profitable an investment will be. Probably the company will make a profit with its investment if the national income will grow. The higher the growth of the future national income (Y future), the higher is the probability of a satisfactory return on the money spent for capital investments.

Therefore Keynes introduces the following function into his model:

4. I = f (i, y Future) (Capital investments are a function of the prevailing interest rates and the future national income.)

Of course, the future national income is not a certified number. It's an estimate. Often the investors take their clues from the past and extrapolate the current trend. The estimate reflects the optimism or pessimism of the investor. So in Keynes's game, investment is the wild card.

As vague as the determining factors of capital investment are, as fixed are the factors which determine the level of consumption, according to Keynes. He assumes that all people have a certain "propensity to consume" (s) and a "propensity to save" (c), meaning that they spend a certain percentage of their income for their living expenses and a certain percentage for their savings.

5. $C = cY$

6. $S = sY$

As in Schumpeter's world, all changes in the economy are triggered by the unpredictable capital investments. When a certain amount of spending for investment occurs (dI), the effects on the gross national product can be calculated by inserting equation 5 into equation 1:

$dY = c \times dY = dI$, which means that

$dY - c \times dY = dI$, which means that

$dY \times (1/c) = dI$, which means that

$dY = dI / (1-c)$

Let's assume that the additional investment amounts to $dI = \$100$ and that people's propensity to consume is $c = 0,9$. The result is an increase of GNP of $dY = \$1,000$.

Of their additional income of $1,000, people save $S = sY = 1/10 \times 1,000 = 100$. The additional investments of $100 therefore generate savings of $100 with the effect that the condition for equilibrium $I = S$ is fulfilled. Macroeconomically, all investment finance themselves.

The same process—only in the opposite direction—takes place when the business sector reduces its investments. When capital investments shrink by $dl = -\$100$, the national income is diminished by $dY = -\$1,000$ and the amount of savings is reduced by $dS = -\$100$.

The sequences which lead to a new equilibrium where the total change of savings equals (dS = dI) can be described by arithmetic series. When people consume 90 percent of their additional income (and therefore save 10 percent), an additional investment of $100 has the following ripple effect:

$90 = $81 = 72.9 = 65.61 = 59.049 = 53.1441, etc. until the stimulus peters out and reaches 0. The sum of the series is $dY = dI = \$100 \times 10 = (1\text{-}c)\ \$1{,}000$.

Keynes's model can be compared to a Ping-Pong game where the purchasing power flies back and forth between the demand side of the economy and its supply side. Welcome to the world of Ping-Pong economics!

At the simplest form of the Keynesian Ping-Pong, at the demand side there are two players: the demand for investment goods (I) and the demand for consumer goods (C).

On the supply side, the participants are the producers of the GNP (Y). We are splitting up the producers of GNP into two branches, the producers of investment goods (YI) and the producers of consumer goods (YC), and we add another participant, the price level (P).

The Keynesian Ping-Pong game starts at the demand side with a serve from the buyers of investment goods (I). Let's assume the additional investment is $100. All purchasing power (dI = $100) flies to the supply side to the producers of investment goods. From there the purchasing power bounces back to the demand side and—according to the propensity to consume and to invest—increases the available funds for savings (1) and for consumption (2).

The funds for consumption in our example amount to $90. The purchasing power of that amount jumps to the supply side, where it is picked up by the consumer industry (3). From there the purchasing power of dY = $90 returns to the demand side, where dC = $81 is earmarked for consumption.

The strength and duration of the Ping-Pong game can be measured by the series of numbers described before. The game ends when the additional purchasing power falls to the level of zero and the additional GNP reaches $1,000 and the additional savings reaches 100. The higher the propensity to spend, the higher is the increase of the GNP.

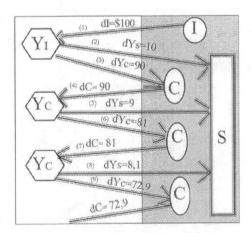

Diagram 3: The perfect Keynesian Ping-Pong game begins with a burst of investments (I). The purchasing power jumps from the demand side to the producers of investment goods (YI) and bounces back to the demand side, increasing savings (S) and consumption (C). Now begins another round of the game with another burst of consumption, reduced in force by the amount saved. The game ends when the consumption does not expand anymore.

The sequence which is illustrated in the graphic above represents what I call the perfect Keynesian game. The game is "perfect" insofar as the additional purchasing power created by capital investments lands exactly there where it has the best impact.

The perfection of the game is due either by the fact that the production capacity has been underutilized and therefore can accommodate the increased demand without strain, or because the additional investment has expanded the production capacities so quickly that the following demand for consumer goods can be fulfilled without creating shortages.

If this condition isn't met and if the supply can't be increased enough to fulfill the additional demand, the imperfect Keynesian game begins.

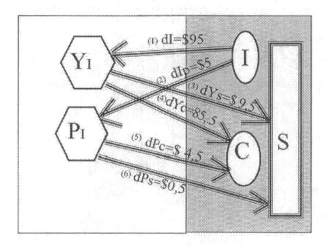

Diagram 4: The imperfect Keynesian Ping-Pong begins with a burst of investment, whose purchasing power is spent for real investment goods (YI) and for an increase of their prices (PI).

The perfect game turns imperfect when not all of the purchasing power lands at the real production (Y) and some of it (or may be even all of it) goes into price increases (6).

This can happen when the demand for investment goods leads to price increases for investment goods. Another possibility is that the increase in the demand for consumer products can't be met because of bottlenecks in the consumer industry. This is how Keynes explains the phenomenon of inflation.

Disinflation (retreating inflation rates) and deflation (reductions of the price level) therefore must be due to unused production capacities.

Let's now have a look if we can explain the long waves with the help of the Keynesian model. It is obvious that Schumpeter's version of the long cycle can't be explained by Keynes because the increase in economic activity in Schumpeter's world is always connected with an increase in inflation. Schumpeter disregards the possibility of a perfect Keynesian game.

In Schumpeter's world, business activity peaks, and the economy grows at a diminishing rate while inflation goes down. Schumpeter's curve of the long wave is based on the assumption that the economic process always takes the form of an imperfect Keynesian game.

In my version of the long wave, a perfect Keynesian game is taking place in phase 1 of the cycle (recovery and expansion). It is an increase of the demand which pulls the economy out of the depression, setting in motion a perfect Ping-Pong game.

At first glance, we might think that phase 2 could be explained by the Keynesian method also. After all, it seems plausible that the expansion of the economy results in shortages. The production apparatus might be too small to generate enough output. Labor might be short in supply, and the demand for raw material may outstrip supplies, turning the perfect Ping-Pong game into an imperfect one. Since the inflationary upswing is stretching over many years, the shortages of labor, raw materials, and production facilities must deteriorate more and more if an imperfect Keynesian game is to continue. But such a development would contradict the tendencies inherent in the capitalist system. Of course, shortages of all kinds are possible in the capitalist economy, but they are overcome over time, as rising prices attract more producers.

Furthermore, the notion of an unfolding imperfect Keynesian game at the turning point to the second phase is contradicted by other features of the inflationary upswing, as I see it. Economic growth continues but at a slower rate as at the end of phase 1 the level of employment goes down (unemployment rises), which doesn't fit into a scenario of an overheating economy.

In phase 2, inflation and unemployment appear together. This cannot be explained either by the concept of an imperfect Keynesian game. Later we will see that the increasing inflation during this phase is not the result of shortages but the result of overabundance.

The Keynesian model can't explain either why the trend line of prices at the turning point after the end of phase 2 is going downward. It could be argued that producers reduce their investments because the existing capacities are either sufficient or too high. This would mean that phase 3 is shaped by an imperfect Keynesian game, this time with a negative bent. But this interpretation doesn't fit because in the third phase of my version of the long waves, the upswing continues while inflation recedes. This combination of positive growth and diminishing inflation begs for an explanation, which I will provide later.

The depression in phase 4 could be explained as an imperfect Keynesian game triggered by dwindling capital investments, which weaken GNP and force prices downward.

But overall, the Keynesian approach doesn't provide much help in explaining the long waves of my design. This is so because of Keynes's limited selection of factors determining the economic process. Of course, no model can ever capture the full complexity of the capitalist economy. Every model is an abstraction, which only takes into account the factors which are relevant for the purpose of the model. The main purpose of Keynes's model was to show that flexible interest rates do not automatically put the economy into a stable equilibrium and that the wild card of capital investments is the decisive factor, as additional investments make the GNP grow, generating the savings, which are necessary to finance the additional investment. Here Keynes succeeded in a brilliant way, and this is his lasting contribution to the dismal science of economics.

As elegant as Keynes's model is, it can't be considered a "general theory," as Keynes claimed. His model has four shortcomings which significantly limit the scope of the insight, which can be derived from it. Here are the shortcomings:

1. The role which the banks are playing in the economic process is not appreciated enough.

In the mind of Keynes, the investors themselves determine which investments are taken and they decide the size of the bank credit, which they need to finance the investment. Very much like in Schumpeter's world, the banks play only a passive role. But every investor knows that things are not that simple and that banks play a significant role in the selection of investment projects.

2. The tautology of I = S

Keynes defines investments as expenses for the purposes of investment financed by savings. And he defines savings as the funds which are used for investments. This is like saying that a duck is a duck.

In reality, savings are not only used for investments but for consumption, since banks provide consumer credit. Keynes's model makes it necessary to subtract the amount of consumer credit from the saving pool, which leaves us with an item, which could be called net savings. By taking account of net savings only, the streams of funds used for consumer credit become invisible.

3. The missing inclusion of old assets like stocks and real estate

Since Keynes was foremost interested in the process which makes the GNP expand or shrink, he uses in his model only the components which directly affect the national income. He overlooks the fact that people may use their income or may use credit to buy items which are not components of the GNP. If somebody buys an old house for the same price the owner paid, the transaction affects the GNP not at all. But for the banker, who provided the credit, the transaction is worth the consideration. It is not unimportant either that the sale of the house has made the former owner more liquid than before, which may entice him to some spending.

If the sale price for the house is higher than the purchase price paid by the owner, the latter makes a profit, which affects the GNP. Keynes's model leaves transactions like this in the dark, shutting out some of the forces which shape the economy.

The same applies to the stock market, which played no role in the Keynesian world.

Richard Nixon's affirmation that "we are all Keynesians now" is true in the sense that almost everyone who thinks in macroeconomic turns uses Keynes's model as a basis for his thinking and, therefore, has no tool at his disposal to link the development at the stock market and at the real estate market for old houses to the productive economy.

4. Money is not invisible

Another shortcoming of Keynes's model is its misconception of the role which money is playing in the economy. As a concrete item, money doesn't even appear in his model. Its existence becomes apparent only indirectly because interest rates are considered to be a contributing factor to the level of capital investments. But here we are dealing with credit, which in our view certainly is not the same as money. Keynes explains the strange invisibility of money in his model by the fact that the model describes the real economic process, which is covered by a monetary "veil." In Keynes's mind, money is just a *numeraire*, an abstract way to calculate the worth of real products.

Isn't it amazing that this interpretation of money is accepted by most economists? This treatment of money may appear plausible when we are dealing with paper money, which seems to have no inherent value. But what about money made out of gold or other precious metal? Shouldn't a "general theory" include the possibility that the money used has value in itself?

Keynes considered gold as "the barbaric metal." By ignoring it, he gave up the opportunity to examine the effects it has on the economy. He therefore could not see how the replacement of gold coins by bank notes changed the whole economic process.

Chapter 3

At the Beginning There Was the Money

"Money matters," Milton Friedman told us again and again. Truer words were never spoken. Indeed, money is important. But it isn't only the quantity of money as Friedman and his followers were thinking. The *quality* of money is important as well, as we will recognize soon.

Considering the importance of money, it is astounding how little the great economists thought about its nature. I mentioned already that Keynes considered it as an abstract device to measure the "underlying" real goods and services.

This characterization is shared by the monetarists, even though they consider the quantity of money in circulation as highly important. History has proven Friedman's main tenet as false. The velocity of money is not stable, as he claims. Therefore, holding steady the growth of the money supply doesn't translate into a steady growth of the gross national product. In 1979, the U.S. Federal Reserve Bank submitted itself to the monetarist codex of behavior and started to focus on meeting certain targets of monetary growth and letting interest rate float accordingly. At first this meant that the growth of the money supply had to be restricted sharply by imposing very high interest rates.

In the following years, the words *money supply* became part of the vocabulary of the American TV audience. There was no news program which didn't inform the viewers of the latest changes in the growth rate of the money supply and its consequences for the stock market. Similar to the augurs who once poked into the entrails of birds for clues about the future, the analysts of the brokerage houses examined the numbers of the monetary supply, which enabled them to utter profound observations about the economy. Whoever wanted to be taken seriously enough to participate in the economic debate had to be knowledgeable about the different concepts for measuring the money supply. Being able to discern the meaning of M1, M2, and M3 was a must.

Like the Hula-Hoop craze, the obsession with the money supply peaked, and soon the topic was out of fashion. Then Federal Reserve chairman Paul Volcker decided to end the adherence to certain targets of the money supply, and the Federal Reserve returned to its traditional policy of fixing interest rates at a level consistent with its goal of reining in inflation.

Milton Friedman deserves our gratefulness, though, for letting us know how important the phenomenon "money" is. I wholeheartedly agree: money matters. But what matters is not only the *quantity* of money, but also its *quality*.

For those who like to place theories in categories, I offer the label "qualitative monetarism" for my creed. The term is supposed to indicate that the quality of the ruling monetary system affects the individuals and their behavior in a fundamental way and determines the course of the economic process.

We get a measure of the quality of today's monetary system by observing the changes it underwent through the centuries. The true nature of money reveals itself when we imagine its creation. The introduction of money into the life of mankind happened a long time ago before there was any recorded history, and so we have no record of its invention or its inventor.

But it is easy to imagine when and why it took place. It must have happened at the stage of economic development when the first steps of partition of labor took place. The members of some clans or tribes surely began this process by bartering their products. They may have given each other credit to facilitate the trade. But no later when they tried to extend the trade to other tribes they surely must have recognized that giving credit is a risky business, requiring mechanisms to record the credit and enforce repayment. Surely they must have been frustrated by the difficulties in swapping some quantities of the items they produced against the desired quantities of the products, which they were lacking. At this point, surely one smart person must have had the idea that it may be profitable to produce some wares which were considered desirable by most people. Soon, someone is specializing in the production of items which could be used as medium for trading. It may have been jewelry first. But soon it became obvious that the most suitable products for the purpose of trading were pieces of precious metal, whose weight and grade of purity was guaranteed by a trusted institution: gold and silver coins proved to be the perfect currency since the metal didn't rust or rot, it could be transported easily, its content could be portioned off precisely, and its intrinsic value was relatively stable because of the metal's scarcity.

These coins constitute real money—there is nothing fake about it. There is no doubt that real money is not just an abstractum. Neither is money just a commodity. **Money is a product.**

Characterizing money as a product may appear to you as a platitude. Still, this trite interpretation of money offers fundamental insights which have been overlooked by the greatest economists.

Of course, money is not a product like all others. It is a product of greatest importance. **The production of money is the beginning of the economic process in any economy based on the partition of labor.** Without money, the economy can't function. Money was created to accommodate humanity's urge for the partition of labor.

As we think of money as a product, we easily come to an understanding of the one essential trait of it: **like any other product, it is created by the use of raw material and labor, and therefore, its production generates incomes totaling the face value of each piece of money.**

And here we have one of the main reasons economies based on a monetary system of coins (or ingots) of gold (or silver or any other precious metal) had a very high stability: **the system comes with a built-in employment program and an income-distribution program.**

A large part of the created money was fetched by those who found the gold. It could happen that someone found a lump of gold and got rich overnight. But most of the gold was quarried in mines. In the original economy, the miners are paid in gold coins. Additionally, the operator of the mine had to pay the landowner for the lease of the property if he didn't own it himself.

A crucial role in the creation of the money was played by the mint because all owners of coins needed assurance that their content had a certain weight and a certain degree of purity.

Of course the sovereign of the country immediately took the responsibility for the weighing and measuring of the metal. This is so because the king during those times was always involved when sources of wealth opened up. Furthermore, it is a legitimate governmental function to guarantee the preciousness of the money in use and discourage and punish cheaters—other than His Majesty himself.

The Royal mint could play two different roles. It could be an enterprise which serviced the mining industry and received a fee for it. Or it could buy the precious metal in order to issue the coins and ingots itself. In most countries, it was the mint which issued the coins, reducing the mining industry to a role of a supplier.

In any case, the role of the Sovereign in shaping and regulating the money supply was crucial.

So the production of gold coins generated a whole set of incomes: the wages of miners and minters, the producers of mining and minting equipment, the lease payments, the minting fees, and the profits of the mining operators and the sovereign owner of the mint. As soon as the recipients of these monies began to spend it, the economy was set in motion. This is it in other words: The production of gold coins created the very same chain of incomes as we know it from Keynes's model.

Original Economy

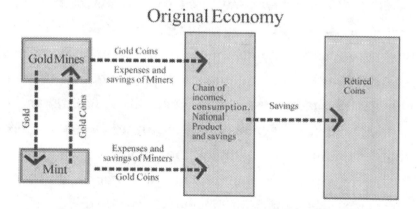

Diagram 5: The linear flow of money in the original economy without banks: gold is extracted from the earth, enters the economy in the form of gold coins, which are ultimately retired as savings.

While in Keynes's world the chain reaction is sparked by a capital investment, in the "barbaric" world of the gold economy it is the production of money which truly makes the world go around.

Therefore the production of $dM = \$100$ makes the economy grow at a rate which is determined by the prevailing average propensity to consume and to save respectively. (Once again the totality of generated income can be calculated by the formula dM divided by the saving rate. If the people save 10 percent of their income, the production of a hundred dollars creates incomes totaling a thousand dollars.)

You may find some irony in the fact that Keynes's model fits the economy based on gold much better than the economy based on central bank money. After all, in the original economy all savings are retired, which is Keynes's assumption as well although that is not the case in the economy based on central bank money.

In the original economy, gold was extracted from the earth, was turned into coins which were handed from one person to another, until it ended up as savings under the mattresses of people and other hiding places. The flow of money was linear, not circular. For that reason, the mint had to produce in each period the same amount of money in order to avoid a shrinking of the economy.

The money which was retired had to be replaced by new money. The mining of precious metals therefore played a key role in the economy. Like the writer Novalis, his contemporaries must have felt that gold and silver had an almost-magical power. Since the economic process in the original economy started with the mining of precious metal for the production of money, gold and silver seemed to be the source of all wealth. This perception conformed to the reality, since all towns close to mines prospered. The California gold rush made many people rich—the most prosperous were not the miners, but those who leased them the land and sold the shovels to dig. But they all owe their riches to the production of money.

Thus we have gotten the following fundamental insights about the nature of real money:

1. The economic process starts with the production of money.
2. The amount of the national income financed by real money is determined by people's propensity to spend their income.
3. If the propensity to spend the income is unchanged, the stability of the economy depends on a continuous, stable production of money.
4. In each given period, the accumulated savings grow by the amount of the newly produced money, creating a monetary overhang.

The original economy, as described, may not have ever existed in its purest form, because

- Some trades may have been conducted through barter.
- The sale of bigger objects, like real estate, may have required some sort of credit financing.
- The money saved didn't always stay in the piggy bank forever but was spent eventually.
- The need for liquidity may have required more coins, slowing down the economic process and reducing national income.

If there ever existed an original economy in the purest form that was shaped by the linear flow of money, it probably didn't exist for long as surely, at one point in time, moneylenders must have emerged, which gradually changed the nature of the monetary system.

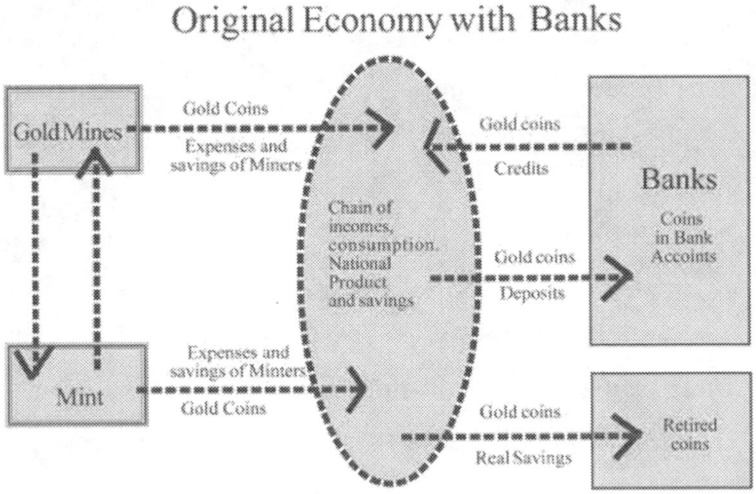

Original Economy with Banks

Diagram 6. As soon as banks begin to operate, parts of the produced gold coins are recycled. The linear flow of money in the pure original economy is turned partially into a circular flow. This is the first step of the gradual demonetization of money.

Indeed, the emergence of banks already changed the quality of the money. People stopped hoarding their savings at home. Instead they gave it to the bank for safekeeping. The interest rate the bank paid made it worthwhile. Of course, not everyone made the switch at once. The ascendance of the banks to their current role took centuries. But moneylenders existed already in biblical times. Powerful banks that financed the wars of the kings existed already in the Middle Ages. But their clientele were the nobility and members of the class of wealthy merchants and manufacturers.

Let us assume once again that the mint produces gold coins worth $100. If the miners and miners deposit their income at bank accounts, the banks have become the means to provide a credit worth of another $900, if they keep reserves of 10 percent. Thanks to the recycling of the coins by the banks, the same amount of money produced by the mint now generates an additional national income of $900. This means that instead of a hundred gold coins, only 52.36 gold coins are needed to generate a national income of 1000. In reality the impact of the banks is far bigger. As more and more people use the services of the bank, money spent hardly leaves the banking sector, which means that the amount of money which the banks have at their disposal has grown much, much more. Any book on banking theory tells you how to calculate the banking multiplicator, which lets you calculate how the banks, by their mere existence, create huge amounts of money.

Which means that from the moment when the banks began to play a role, only a fraction of the original gold coins was needed to finance a national product of $1,000. The "demonetization" of money or the "de-golding" of it had started, even though the gold coins were still the currency in use.

It is easy to imagine how this change of the monetary system effected the mining industry and the mint, which lost much most of its power. As diagram 6 shows, the former linear flow of money turned into a cycle as soon as people began to use their deposit slips as money substitutes.

The receipts for deposits of gold coins were the predecessors of today's banknotes. At this stage in the development of the monetary system, the size of the national product was still dependent on the production of gold coins by the mint, but the circulation of the banknotes practically reduced the gold content of the total currency due to the ability of the banks to issue credit "out of thin air."

The banknotes reduced the amount of gold which had to be produced each year in order to keep the economy going. The built-in employment program for miners and minters became smaller. Resources used for the production of money were freed for other more productive use. On the other hand, the stability of the system had been weakened. Otherwise the structure of the original economy remained the same.

All this changed when the banks accepted banknotes as deposits on their accounts and began issuing loans denominated in banknotes.

This meant a huge step forward in the process of the demonetization of money.

But in the mind of people, the banknotes remained only a substitute of the real thing—until all banks honored not only their own notes, but also the notes of their competitors as well. The creation of a central bank made it possible to issue uniform banknotes, which helped to turn the banknotes into the generally accepted means of payment.

Until recently, all owners of central bank notes still had the right to get the notes replaced by gold coins. People who wanted to save the coins the old-fashioned way—under the mattress or in a vault—had to do without the interest payment the banks were offering, and they had take measures against the possible theft of the coins.

These disadvantages of hoarding gold coins had to be compared to the risks of keeping the money as deposits in bank accounts. After all, banks are engaged in the risky lending business, and when they go bankrupt the deposits may vanish. By creating a central bank, the bankers took an important step to make their individual institutes safer because in a case of a liquidity crisis they now could count on credit by the central bank. The central bank is, therefore, above all a tool to make the demonetization of money acceptable to the public.

The funds which the central bank could provide were limited in quantity only by the requirement to hold a certain minimum of reserves in gold. When these requirements were lifted, the last strings which tied the central bank money to gold were cut, and the creation of credit had no fixed boundaries anymore.

The monetary system of the so-called gold-standard was an attempt to provide the patina of gold to central bank money. Theoretically the convertibility of the dollar into gold could provide a measure of stability as the central bank had to rein in its credit expansion in order to stabilize the market price of gold. Inflation had to be stopped. But the resulting slowdown of economic growth and the increase in unemployment came as a high price for maintaining the convertibility of the dollar to gold. The gold standard therefore was doomed.

Economy with Banks issuing Receipts of Deposits
used as money substitute

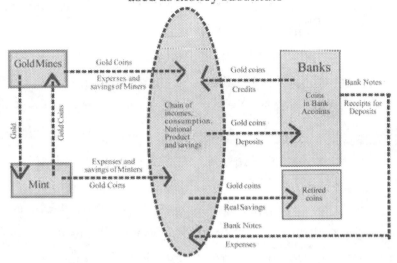

Diagram 7: When bank customers begin to use their deposit slips
as substitute money, the linear flow of money is weakened and the
circular flow increases.

It should be acknowledged that the gold standard was a
form of cover-up of the fact that the banknotes really only
had a small gold content. The production of one hundred
gold dollars, which in the original economy set in motion the
creation of a national product of one thousand dollars even
under the regime of the gold standard, now permitted the
national product to grow at an exponential rate. The availability
of money ceased to be a limiting factor of growth.

Only the bank's requirement of reserves in central bank
money and some "leaks" in the everlasting flow of money
kept a lid on the credit expansion.

It was only logical that the convertibility of the central
bank money had to be ended. Since that happened, gold
plays hardly any role in the monetary system of the world

anymore. As a consequence, the role of the mint was diminished substantially. The U.S. mint is still in operation, but it produces only change. The coins are made out of light metal, and the nominal value of the coins has no relation to their metal content. The production of the paper money, as well as the money created by entries in the ledger by computer transactions, is controlled by the banks. That's where the big money is.

The importance of this development can hardly be overestimated. Without the liberation from the yoke of the gold, the capitalistic economies could never have blossomed as much as they did. Gold's diminished importance had profound economic and social implications. The landowning

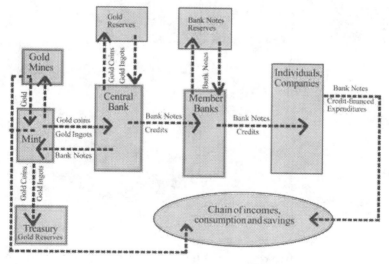

Diagram 8: The central bank facilitates the creation of credit, accelerating the demonetization of money.

class, which owned the mining rights, lost most of its wealth and influence to the bankers and entrepreneurs, who now could produce all the money they needed. The monetary evolution thus fostered the decline of feudalism and the ascendance of the bourgeoisie. The prevailing central bank money owes its existence to the urge of breaking the constraints of the gold money due to the short supply of its main ingredient. By in its origin, today's central bank money is counterfeit

Economy with Central Bank Money
with Zero Gold coverafe

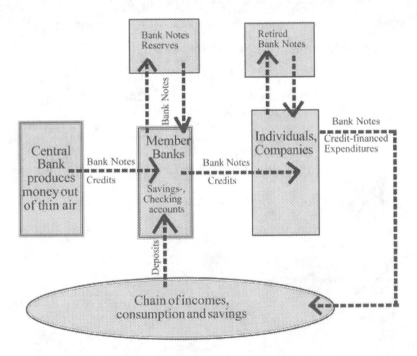

Diagram 9: When the central bank issues bank notes, which can be deposited in bank accounts, the demonetization of money makes a big leap forward. When the central bank doesn't back up the banknotes with gold anymore, the demonetization of money is complete.

money. The banks behaved like innkeepers who dilute the wine offered to the customers more and more by water and, finally, serve only water with a faint taste of wine.

But since the "fake" money filled a need, it was generally accepted. The central bank, whose role it is to perfect the "forgery," is a highly respected institution, which is often praised as the "guardian of the currency."

Its function is barely understood by the public. But when the critical moment comes and the economy descends into the depression, it becomes obvious that the central bank of today has the same function as it always had. It helps the member banks to issue loans with very little capital and make money on interest rates which their clients can only pay if their projects succeed. It's a gamble. The smaller the reserves are, which the member banks have to keep, the more funds they can use and the more risky becomes the game.

Diagram 8 shows how, over time, the linear stream of the produced real money has turned into an ever-swelling circle of substitute money. The banks have become masters in recycling the money faster and faster, thus expanding the total amount of funds which they can use. The faster the money can be recycled, the smaller is the amount of new money, which they have to borrow from the central bank. The current flooding of the populace with credit card debt shows that the banks are still perfecting the credit machine.

Since the financing of the national product doesn't require the production of gold coins anymore, the economic process no longer begins with the creation of incomes. The continuing "employment program" (for the miners and minters) has been abolished. One pillar, on which the edifice of the economy used to rest, has been dismantled. The once modest house of the economy has been remodeled into a skyscraper—without the pillars, which provide stability. This is so because in an economy based on central bank money, the economic process begins with the granting of credit. Therefore, the economy can only function if the banks are able to make loans. If they can't, there is no flow of new incomes which can sustain the economy.

Furthermore, it makes a big difference whether the economic process begins with the creation of income or with the granting of credit, because **people spend their income differently than the money obtained by credit.** The recipients of incomes can spend their money as it pleases them. Credit usually is with strings attached. Large amounts of credit are only given for the purchase of specified items or for a defined purpose. Whoever wants to get a loan has to convince the bank that the project to be financed generates a sufficient stream of income which makes it possible for the debtor to pay the interest and pay back the loan.

For the bank, any decision to grant a loan is tied to the question whether the debtor-to-be can offer enough security. Financing the purchase of a building gives the bank the chance to attach a mortgage to the property, which guarantees the bank the ownership of the piece of real estate if the interest and the principal is not paid according the loan agreement. In most cases, the bankers will only grant the loan if the value of that property is likely to increase over time and/or if they come to the conclusion that the income of the debtor or the value of his assets will be sufficient.

Sometimes the security for a loan rests in the personality of the debtor or in the character of the institution which applies for the credit. In such cases the bankers are confident that the debtor will use the money wisely to enhance his future incomes.

Here lies the dynamic built into the monetary system based on central bank money. Money is created by granting credit on the assumption that incomes will grow and that the debtors will prosper.

Within the framework of this monetary system, the economy is condemned to grow. If it doesn't, the stability of the economy is in jeopardy. So the banks' fortunes are tied to the fortunes of their debtors.

Which influence do the bankers have on the development of the economy? Keynes and Schumpeter believed that the bankers are just marionettes of the companies and entrepreneurs. Marionettes who eagerly provide the loans needed for the investments of the true masters of the land, the entrepreneurs. But we will see that this interpretation of the role of the banker is very incomplete. We will see that the decisions of the bankers have a vast impact on the economy. It is true, though, that the banks' choices are limited. They can only provide loans to other people's projects. Their choice is to provide the credit—or rather not. But since the banks can only make a profit by making loans, they find it very difficult to wind down their activity, when in hindsight they should have done so. The bankers are acting under constraints, which results in predictable decisions. They display patterns of behavior, and those patterns are shaping the form of the long waves.

Chapter 4

The Source of the Big Wave

In order to understand the nature of the quality of central bank money and grasp its impact on the economy, we once again have to return to the original economy. Let us observe more closely the economic process taking place when the money is made out of pure gold. Let us watch how the Ping-Pong game is played under these conditions.

While Keynes and all the others differentiate the actors on the demand side of the playing field by the purpose of the expenses—consumption or investment—we differentiate the players according to the origin of the money. This messes up the elegant simplicity of Keynes's model. But it frees us from constraints which make us think unproductively. Because if you differentiate the demand according to the purpose of the expenses, you end up with tautologies. What honey is there to lick when the model is based on the truism, that the expenses for investments are used to purchase investment goods and the expenses for consumption are spent for consumer goods?

We are placing three actors on the demand side of the playing field:

o   Income-financed demand (DIncome),
o   Credit-financed demand (DCredit), and
o   Asset-financed demand (DAsset)

On the supply side of the playing field, we are placing the well-known Keynesian actors:

o   The real national product Y and
o   its price level P.

These two actors on the supply side constitute the Y-component of the economy, which consists of newly created products and services.

But besides the Y-component, we now introduce an X-component, which consists of the existing assets—the old stuff, which constitutes the wealth of people.

The X-component consists of many wonderful things like paintings, jewelry, carpets, used cars, and much, much more. But we focus on the two main parts of the X-component:

-   the value of stocks
    XStocks and its price level
    PXStocks
    and
-   the value of existing real estate
    XReal Estate and
    its price level
    PXReal Estate.

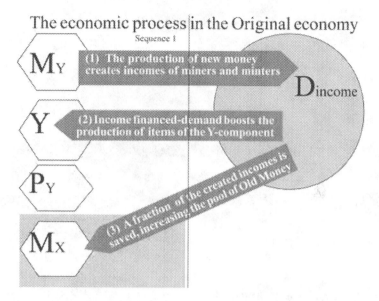

Diagram 9

In the original economy, the economic process begins with the production of new money (My) in the form of gold coins (1) creating incomes of miners and minters. The created income is mostly spent (2) on items which make up the national product. The rest is saved (3), creating a pool of old money (Mx). The ripple effect of the gold production peters out when all new money has become old money. The economic process might end here. More newly produced money will repeat the process.

Possibly, some people will mobilize parts of the old money (5) in order to buy real estate (6) or stocks (7). The sellers of those assets will become more liquid (8). The amount of the old money remains the same, only the ownership of has changed.

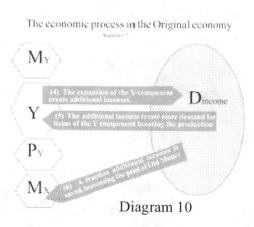

Diagram 10

The economic process in the Original economy
Sequence 3

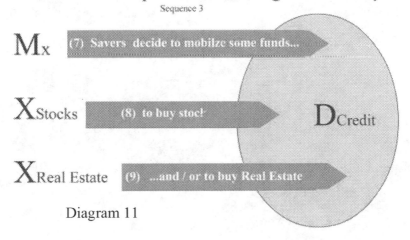

M_x (7) Savers decide to mobilze some funds...

X_{Stocks} (8) to buy stock D_{Credit}

$X_{Real\ Estate}$ (9) ...and / or to buy Real Estate

Diagram 11

There are more actors to watch at the supply side. One is the new money

(My)

and the old money

(Mx).

Since we consider money to be a concrete object and not just a veil hovering over the transactions, we can abandon the construct of abstract purchasing power, which jumps from one side to the other. Instead, we can observe real pieces of money moving back and forth.

We know that in the original economy the economic process begins with the production of new gold. So the economic process starts on the supply side. The money produced (My) flows entirely to those who are involved in the money production and now have the income to spend according to their wishes. (See arrow 1). These people spend most of the money on items which are part of the real national product (Y, arrow 2). The remaining coins they save by hiding them under the mattress (arrow 3).

The money spent turns into income of the producers of the national product (arrow 4), which used their income according their preferences. For the sake of simplicity, we assume that the farmers, bakers, masons, and other producers of components of the national product use their money the same way as the miners and minters. A perfect Keynesian game is taking place.

Introducing the X-component into this simple but stable economy doesn't necessarily disturb the perfect Keynesian play. Of course, purchases of old assets like stocks and old houses take place. Assuming these purchases are financed out of savings, old money flows to the demand side (D) asset (arrow 5) and is spent for old real estate (arrow 6) and stocks (arrow 7). If the sellers of these assets save their liquidated assets (arrow 10), only a restructuring of assets takes place without consequences for the national product. If the liquidated assets are used for purchasing goods and services (arrow 11),

The economic process in the Original economy

Sequence 4

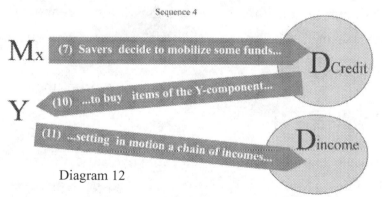

Diagram 12

the Y-component expands. Under these "perfect" conditions, the monies which went to the X-component have no effects which could distort the economic development.

Things are different under the conditions of an imperfect Keynesian play. Various circumstances could cause an increase in the price level (Py) of the Y-component. For example, due to bad weather the harvest of wheat could have been diminished. Wheat prices would rise, partially at the expense of the prices of other products because people would allocate their income-financed expenses differently. Additionally people would temporarily tap into their savings in order to get their share of wheat. Since the producers can't increase the supply of wheat quickly, the demand (D) asset financed by old money drives up the wheat prices even further.

This shows that even in the original economy an accelerating inflation is possible. But the funds for the speculation in wheat are limited by the size of the accumulated savings. If the next harvest of wheat is plentiful, the prices of the grain will recede, the speculation ends, and the economy returns to its regular path determined by the yearly production of gold coins.

Keeping the production of gold coins steady is the main condition for the functioning of the original economy. An increase in the supply of gold coins is as problematic as a shortage of them.

If the production of new money falls short of the regular amount, the real output of the economy doesn't necessarily have to shrink. If everybody lowers the prices of their product, no harm is done. But these adjustments cause frictions and discontent. Since the value of each gold coin increases in times of deflation, some people may hoard more than usual and prices may shrink further. As some prices may stick to their old level, depending on the level of competition, a decrease of the money supply may result in a shrinking of the Y-component of the economy.

An increase in the production of gold coins creates additional income. If the manufacturers and farmers can expand their output sufficiently, the real national product, the Y-component, will grow. But if these favorable conditions are not existing, bottlenecks will develop and soon too much money will chase too few.

Now let's have a look at what happens when the banks get into the picture and change the flow of money from a linear flow into a circle. Two things now change. The supply of money is suddenly abundant, and it is channeled into the economy by means of bank loans. The situation somehow looks similar than the one we described for the case of an increase in the gold production of the original economy. But the differences should not be overlooked. In the original economy, the increase in the money supply is limited by the scarcity of gold and the new money enters the economy as income. Now as the bank recycles the money, the money supply is almost totally flexible, adjusting to the needs of the businesses. And since the money is created in the form of credit, it isn't spent on consumer products but on capital investments, which create the production facilities to meet the growing demand.

We now have entered the first phase of the long waves. In this phase, everything seems to work fine. It's all the bank's fault—even the stunning increase of prosperity in this phase is the "fault" of the banks, which are feeding the industries which produce the goods and services that are most in demand. Contrary to the situation in the original economy, there are

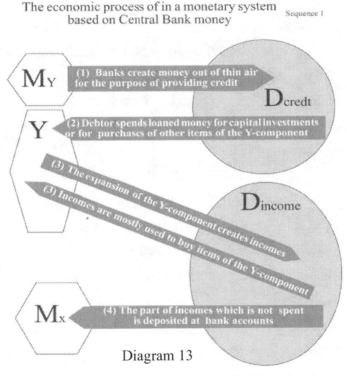

Diagram 13

In an economy with central bank money, the recovery from depression begins at the turning points (T44) with the liquidation of assets. New money is mobilized to fund the purchase of bankrupt production facilities, real estate, and stocks. The liquidity creates asset-financed demand for components of the national product, which in turn creates income-financed demand for items of the national product.

The recovery may be weak, but it sets the stage for a full-fledged expansion as soon as new money is mobilized to fund credit-financed demand for capital investments and other parts of the economy's Y-component. As long as this perfect Keynesian game continues, the expansion continues without inflationary side effects.

ample funds available for producers who want to build up their capacities of making more of the existing products or new products they hope to sell. In this phase, the textbook of great successful banking and visionary entrepreneurs and growing companies is written. Most of the money follows the rules of the perfect Keynesian game. It enters the economy in the form of credit for the financing of capital investments and it then turns into a sequence of incomes, consumption, and savings.

Since the production capacities are growing, productivity is increasing. There is hardly any inflation and almost no unemployment. In this phase, people begin to think that the problems of the capitalist system have been solved and that the economy can only grow and that every industrious person can make good money. This is the time when successful entrepreneurs look like the heroic figures out of Schumpeter's world. Yes, their success is stunning. But with all the respect they deserve, it should be mentioned that during this period the entrepreneurs often can't go wrong. The companies can concentrate on making the production efficient. Because of the huge pent-up demand, many products sell by themselves.

During this phase, the producers don't need marketing gurus. It is obvious that consumers who started out with a bicycle soon would want a motorcycle and would then aspire to have a car. First, people would enjoy more and better food. Soon they would be looking for fancier clothing, furniture, and plush carpets. The construction industry of course is booming. People want more living space, a house with a garden instead of a cramped apartment in the city. The new prosperity feels like a miracle. But actually, what's going on is quite predictable for anybody thinking in terms of the long waves. Predictably, the construction industry and the auto industry are the mainstays of the expansion because the value of their products is bigger than most other products and because consumers can easily finance them by debt. The banks provide cheap mortgages and loans for the purchases of automobiles. Houses and cars, from the perspective of the bankers, have the distinction that they can be attached with a financial instrument. These products fulfill the bankers' need for some sort of security as they can seize them in the case of a distressed loan.

While the conditions prevailing in the first phase of the long wave shapes all market economies in the world, in each country the upswing has a different character. You see, when we refer to the world economy, we are not talking about one homogenous entity. The world economy consists of a multitude of national economies which differ vastly. Only a few countries used to have a diversified industrial sector. Other countries have little manufacturing but plenty of mining, oil-extraction, or farming. From each of these countries come different impulses according to the stage of their own development. But no matter how industrialized a country and how sophisticated their banking sector is, they all get sucked into the maelstrom of the long waves because of their interactions by the imports and exports of goods and of capital.

Of course, people are not aware that the current conditions of the economies are shaped by the long waves. People feel that the current situation lasts forever. That's why they follow the same pattern of behavior. Companies continue to borrow money in order to expand production capacities for popular products, expecting that the demand for the products will continue to grow. But there comes the time when the demand stops growing. Suddenly some production facilities stand idle. The turning point has arrived. The wonderful first phase of the long waves is over.

Chapter 5

The Source of Inflation

The second phase of the long waves is characterized by accelerating inflation rates, chronic unemployment, increasing prices of real estate and raw materials, stagnating prices of stocks, and reduced and unstable growth of the national product.

The first question is this: what triggered the inflation?

The second question is this: why does the inflation continue and even accelerate?

Splitting the analysis of inflation in this way makes sense, because the factors which set in motion the "cyclical inflation," as I call this type of the rise of the price index typical for the second phase of the long waves, are not necessarily the same as the forces which nourish the uptick of prices and let inflation spiral upward.

Without making this distinction, the understanding of the inflation during this phase would be incomplete at best. People who trust their common sense would of course argue that inflation must have been caused by the shortness of supplies. Others may feel that the increased costs because of higher wages must have been the cause. These factors could indeed explain why prices start to raise after the turning point from the first phase to the second phase of the long waves. But this doesn't explain why inflation during this phase persists and rises. After all, shortages come and go. And producers in capitalist economies are often capable of reducing the pressure of costs by an increase of productivity and other measures to circumvent the high costs of labor. Today's shortages turn into abundance tomorrow. Such is the nature of the modern capitalist industrial economy.

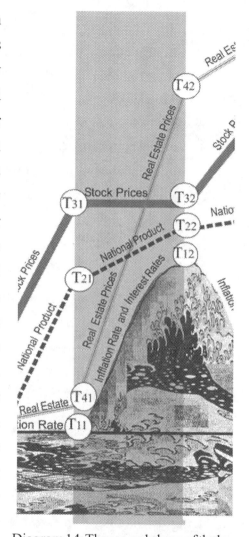

Diagram 14: The second phase of the long waves begins when at T11 the products and services which are part of the Y-component become more expensive. The inflation rate for these items is surpassed by steep price increases for real estate and commodities like oil, starting at T31. Beginning at T21 the growth of the Y-component is leveling off. Stock prices begin to stagnate at T41.

A shortage of raw materials seems to be a logical explanation on why inflation starts. After all, during the preceding phase of expansion, the demand for raw materials has risen in proportion with the increasing output. This answer may satisfy all those who are worried by the limited supplies of natural resources. But at least until now the limitations in the production of commodities have been overcome. Temporary shortages may cause inflationary impulses, and as most industries are trying to pass on their increased costs, there could be a sizable increase of the price level.

But I have come to the conclusion that the beginning of cyclical inflation is not so much caused by too much demand chasing too few raw materials, but by a lack of demand and unused production capabilities. The increase of unemployment is one of the indicators that some existing production capabilities are left unused.

The sudden increase in unemployment at the beginning of the second phase is the result of a severe recession, which typically ends the expansion of the first phase.

During the recession, prices usually go down. And at first this happens too during this recession. But as soon as the recession is overcome, inflation rises while the increase of employment doesn't suffice to reach full employment.

For me, cyclical inflation and cyclical unemployment are ugly twins. Their birth can be explained by the most important effect of modern industrial production: the so-called economies of scale. Mass production makes it possible to lower the costs per unit. It requires high capital expenses to put in place the production facilities which reap the benefits of economies of scale to the fullest extent. Luckily, the heavy financial burden which comes with the construction of these highly productive facilities become lighter over time and the more units are produced. As fixed costs spread over a higher number of produced units, the portion of the fixed costs per produced units becomes smaller.

The economies of scale are the foundation of the prosperity which industrialization bestows on all of us. But these economies of scale reverse their effect when the output lags and fewer units are produced. The fixed costs per unit are rising now.

At first, producers may refrain from rising prices. They may even lower them for a while for competitive reasons. But not for long, because mounting losses could jeopardize the existence of producers who take this path. Soon these producers must raise prices if they want to stay in business.

The correlation between increasing unit costs and price increases is strongest in highly competitive markets. Our economic literature tells us that under the condition of total competition, prices equal marginal costs. When productivity goes down due to a decline in output, the fixed costs become a heavier burden, increasing the marginal costs per unit and pushing up prices.

Even in an oligopolistic competition, typical for the auto industry, the correlation between marginal costs and prices is strong. Everybody knows that the auto industry was the first in reaping the benefits of the economies of scale by introducing the assembly line and other methods of saving labor costs. These advantages of mass production required huge investments which burdened the manufacturer with high fixed costs. The benefits of these investments can only be realized by a high degree of utilization of the production facilities.

As demand for automobiles grew during the phase of expansion of the long waves, the companies were able to operate close to total utilization of the production apparatus. This created the best of all worlds as profits were skyrocketing while prices declined, since competition forced the producers to pass on part of the savings to the buyers in the form of lower prices.

This ideal world crumbles as soon as demand slows, as it must, since at one point in time there are only few people left who don't own a car yet. When this happens, big profits turn into big losses quickly. The modern industrial economy therefore has a built-in tendency of rising unit costs and rising prices whenever the output is shrinking.

In this period some producers go bankrupt, some are taken over by stronger competitors. Others survive by honing their production skills and firing the employees which they don't need anymore. It takes a while until the tendency to higher marginal costs is overcome. But the happy times of the expansion phase are gone for good.

The trouble is that it isn't as predictable anymore as it used to be, what kind of products people want to buy. Furthermore, people are now able to save more money. The savings weaken the Y-component while increasing the pool of funds which the banks can use for their lending.

It has become risky. The industrialists may try to improve their products or come up with new ones to satisfy needs which people didn't know they had. Marketing and advertising play a growing role. But success is not guaranteed. The manufacturing business has become complicated and the banks' lending business as well.

But if the banks cannot lend funds, they make no profit. Therefore, they must be relieved to notice that the uptick in inflation has brought new opportunities to them. The

Diagram 15: The origin of cyclical inflation: slumping income-financed demand reduces the production of goods and services with the result of rising costs per unit.

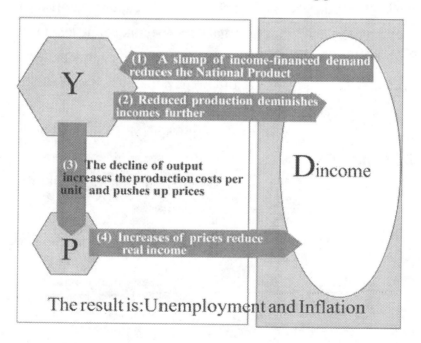

Cyclical inflation   Sequence 1 The Trigger

Y

(1) A slump of income-financed demand reduces the National Product

(2) Reduced production deminishes incomes further

(3) The decline of output increases the production costs per unit and pushes up prices

D income

P

(4) Increases of prices reduce real income

The result is: Unemployment and Inflation

inflationary impulse may be small yet, but nevertheless, the value of existing real assets has increased. Owning real estate looks like a winning strategy now. The rising prices of old houses are an encouragement to build new ones. As the costs of building new houses rises, older houses become more valuable. So the second phase of the long waves gets its direction by what I call an X-game: the bank provides loans for the purpose of buying components of the X-components, assets like existing houses, and raw materials like oil.

Rising real estate prices make the speculation in old houses worthwhile and encourage speculators to use more credit for this purpose. Commodities offer other opportunities for speculation.

Undoubtedly, the most of important raw material is oil. Storing additional oil seems to be difficult. But in fact, it is easier than imagined. When people buy their heating oil earlier than usual because they fear that it will become more expensive, they in fact create additional storage. Also, producers of oil are very sensitive to inflation. They may keep more of the stuff longer in the ground, or as the market is dominated by a monopoly, they may raise oil prices outright. Another conduit for higher prices are the commodity exchanges which provide speculators to gamble on oil and drive up its price. All this is only possible with the help of the banks.

Cyclical inflation   Sequence 2 The acceleration

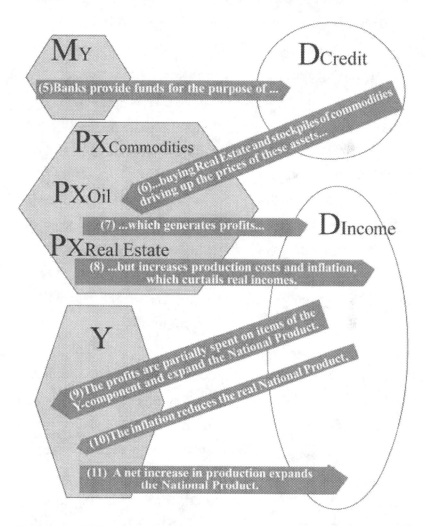

Diagram 16: The increase of unit cost because of lower production numbers results in an uptick of inflation which makes existing assets more valuable, which invites speculators to buy these old assets. Banks are happy to provide credit since the rising prices of these assets provide additional security for the loans.

Fortunately, the increasing prices of old houses make it more profitable to build new ones. As soon as more credit flows into the construction of new houses, a Keynesian game is set in motion, an imperfect one, since the banks are not only financing the real thing, but also the increased prices. Nevertheless, the Y-component begins to expand, which obscures the fact that the new prosperity is based on the speculation that prices will rise further.

Before we render judgment on the character of those bankers who finance their speculation, let's try to put ourselves in their shoes. We have to keep in mind that the banks must provide loans if they want to make any money.

They have to make sure that their debtors are able and willing to pay interest on the loans and eventually will pay back the amount borrowed. The problem is that the dynamic producer who had financed his expansion by bank loans is suffering from a lack of demand for his products and doesn't need more credit. Who else is there, who can need some bank loans? Perhaps the real estate investor who thinks of buying an old building? Or the industrialist who wants to increase his stock of raw materials? Real estate and raw materials seem to be undervalued compared to industrial products and are bound to appreciate in value. Therefore, financing these purchases carries little risks, and so the bankers gladly provide the loans.

They soon realize that they found a new source of profit, because the increase in demand for old houses, oil, metals, and other commodities pushes up their prices. We are dealing here with a case of self-fulfilling prophecies.

The swelling X-component due to the rising price of old houses doesn't have much of a direct impact on the Y-component (the national product). But soon the indirect effects will be felt. The appreciation of the value of the old-housing stock makes new houses more valuable too. This leads to more construction of new houses, which bolsters the Y-component.

More direct is the impact of rising commodity prices, which affect the X-component (increasing the value of existing supplies) and the Y-component, as producers are making more profit. Furthermore, the increasing prices of raw materials are affecting the industries which depend on them. When those industries raise the prices of their products, inflation is taking hold.

The rising prices of old and new houses makes renting living space more expensive too, and this increases the inflationary pressure. A fundamental shift of wealth is now taking place. The winners are the ones who bought real estate early on, the losers are the one who keep in renting or feel obliged to jump on the bandwagon belatedly and pay inflated prices for a piece of real estate.

But the economy as a whole is stimulated by the real estate boom. The wages and profits of the construction industry feed demand for all kinds of products and services, which in turn make the whole Y-component expand.

Even the sectors whose crisis marked the transition from phase 1 of the long waves (expansion) to phase 2 are doing good business again if they adjusted to the changes of the demand structure.

The merriment goes on as long as interest rates increase less than inflation. This lag between inflation rates and interest rates is essential for this phase. For the sake of simplification I decided to consolidate the development of inflation and interest rates into one curve, taking a cue from Schumpeter.

But in a detailed analysis of each of the phases of the long waves, it is necessary to take note of the lags between the development of the price index and the interest rates. Without this lag, the inflationary upswing would crumble.

The gap between the level of interest rates and the level of inflation is due to the fact that the prevailing short-term interest rates are not determined by the financial markets but by the central bank. If the markets would be the determining force, the gap would disappear. But as the central bank doesn't want to abort the economic upswing, it is compelled to keep interest rates lower than the inflation rate. Those who keep money on their bank accounts must endure negative real interest rates. It could be said that the central bank deliberately feeds the inflation during this phase of the long waves. But the central bankers have no other choice. Raising interest rates to the level of inflation would let the economy stagnate or even shrink.

Concerned about the increasing inflation, the central bank may at one point in time ponder if it has to counteract and fight inflation by raising interest rates. The real estate boom would come to a halt as the increased financing costs would reduce sales, and the market value of houses would go down. A recession would interrupt the upswing, unemployment would spread. This is exactly what happened in the seventies.

The economic discussion during that period dwelled on the "trade-off" between inflation and unemployment. I remember that I myself as a young newspaper writer composed thoughtful articles about the necessity to choose between the plague of inflation and the cholera of unemployment. As long as inflation seems to be bearable, policymakers are inclined to choose the plague.

These deliberations were based on the notion that any increase in employment comes with the cost of higher inflation. This theory was condensed into the Phillips curve, which quantified inflationary "cost" in higher output and increased employment. Thinkers in the Keynesian mold had no trouble explaining the inverse relationship between employment and inflation. They argued that any increases in output would be hampered by bottlenecks of the production. So we are once again talking about an imperfect Keynesian game, which we had ruled out as the determining factor of the second phase of the long waves.

Still, the trade-off between inflation and unemployment is a reality during the phase of the inflationary upswing. But its cause cannot be found in the field of production but in the realm of monetary theory.

Once again we have to take into account that within the monetary framework of central bank money, the economy can only grow if the banks are able to make loans. As long as production capacities for parts of the Y-component are still plentiful, banks can only provide more loans if the market value of bankable items is growing in value, improving the chances that the debtors are able to pay the interest and the principal.

By feeding the speculation in real estate and in raw materials and thus giving nourishment to inflation, the banks are prospering again. The economy at large is growing as well. The misallocation of resources by the banks seems to be bearable since the construction industry is growing, converting bank credit into income-financed demand. The rising prices of assets create wealth, which leads to welcome consumer spending.

This could happily go on forever if the inflation would not have the tendency to speed up. At a certain stage an inflation mentality is taking hold, which makes people buy products sooner than later, trying to escape rising prices.

But there comes the time when the public begins to fear the impact of inflation more than the consequences of unemployment, and the central bank is allowed to display its independence by raising interest rates.

As soon as the credit machine slows down, the economy begins to sputter. Of course, the crisis begins in the construction industry, but it spreads quickly to the economy at large. Inflation begins to slow down, and the central bankers have to opportunity to wonder how much unemployment is required to stop inflation and how much unemployment is tolerable.

Soon respectable economists will argue that there is a "natural rate of unemployment" which serves as a kind of buffer against the inflationary effects of the bottleneck. Still, there is a limit for tolerance to the plight of the people who lose their job. When the central bankers have convinced themselves that inflation has been tamed enough, they once again open the spigot of credit by lowering interest rates.

As long as the level of interest rates is still high enough to be lowered substantially, the abundant credit will find its takers who, by their credit-financed spending, pull the economy out of the recession.

There can be several recessions interrupting the inflationary upswing. These recessions are typical patterns of the second phase of the long waves. There is a chance that a recession can't be overcome quickly by the return to easy credit. Then the politicians might resort to deficit spending, which does the trick but saddles the government with a big load of debt. The government then seems to have no other choice than raising taxes—and creating the conditions for "stagflation." Inflation doesn't "buy" much growth and employment anymore.

The inflationary upswing is not an especially good time for the stock market. Sure, the companies may be able to pass on the rising costs to the consumers by increasing the prices of their products. But the real economy is relatively weak, since the banks channel a large part of their credit into inflationary projects. Therefore, the stock market stagnates.

It is in the real estate sector where the action is. Investing in real estate seems to be a sure bet. It is therefore very likely that the second phase of the long waves ends with a big bang caused by the collapse of the speculation in real estates. This can happen when real estate prices have risen to a level where they have lost touch with the underlying economy.

Another scenario could be that the central bank once again engineers a recession by raising interest rates. But this time, the central bank keeps its restrictive credit policy in place until the inflation mentality is really broken. A severe recession marks the end of the inflationary upswing.

It is conceivable though that the central bank continues to make more credit available and let inflation roar. If the central bank follows this path, the end of the inflationary upswing comes only after the money is heavily devaluated and increases in inflation "buy" hardly any real growth anymore. But I consider such a development as an aberration from the typical path of the long waves.

In any case, it can be said that the inflationary upswing ends at the moment when the inflationary mentality has been broken, one way or another.

Chapter 6
The Disinflationary Upturn

Inflation continues as long as the central bank continues to keep interest rates lower than the rate of inflation. As long as the real interest rate (nominal interest rate minus inflation) is negative, it appears to be profitable to buy real estate, precious metals, raw materials, and pieces of art because these items are likely to gain in value. But as soon as the central bank adjusts the interest rates to the level of inflation or even lets them shoot higher, the profitability of such purchases becomes doubtful. Because of the accumulative impact of rising interest rates, due to the large sums to be financed, the impact on real estate prices is felt quickly.

The decline of real estate prices cools the construction boom and slows down the Y-component of the economy. If the central bank withstands the pressure to once again ease the supply of credit, at one point the general inflation rate will crest. Austerity has its rewards! But the success of the fight against inflation comes with the price of a severe recession. The capital markets will only be impressed if the central bank bites the bullet and shows no inclination to change the course even though the increased unemployment and the hardship in many sectors of the economy are testing the resolve of policymakers. Only when the inflation mentality is really, really broken can the next phase of the long waves begin.

Whether the central bank is able and willing to make this happen depends on many factors. Politics plays a big role, and the personality of the central bankers play a role as well. The self-interest of the member banks are to be considered also. After all, the bankruptcy of some of their clients could threaten the very existence of some banks. The hyperinflation in Germany after the First World War shows that there is no automatism regulating the actions of the central bank. But on the other hand, letting a hyperinflation roar must be seen as an aberration from rational behavior.

Therefore, I assume that the central bank at one point in time indeed puts the brakes on and permits a severe recession to take place. How can such a recession, which lets the X-component as well as the Y-component stagnate or even shrink, lead to another upturn? The road is cleared when interest rates have peaked and begin to slide. Lower interest rates increase the value of existing assets like stocks, bonds, and real estate, providing new opportunities for the banks to issue credit.

The trend to lower interest rates must not necessarily begin with a change of monetary policy by the central bank. It can begin at the capital markets for long-term debt. Long-term interest rates do not fully depend directly on the credit policy of the central bank, which is only geared to manipulate short-term interest rates. Long-term interest rates, on the other hand, are heavily determined by inflationary expectations. Therefore, some tangible proof that inflation is slowing triggers a reduction of long-term interest rates and an increase in bond prices.

The central bank may continue to keep short-term interest rates high and let the decline of the long-term rates lift the spirits of traders and producers alike. But it is only a matter of time until the central bank may begin to lower its rates as well.

This depends on the philosophy of the central bankers. Do they attempt to wipe out inflation as quickly as possible, or are they content seeing it recede gradually?

If they choose the radical solution, they risk steering the economy on a rather short road toward the depression. So the rational approach would be to let the price index go down slowly. The higher the peak of inflation and the slower inflation recedes, the longer the period of the disinflationary upswing lasts.

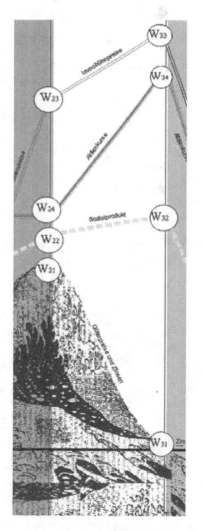

Diagram 16

If the central bank wants to take this gradual approach, it may lower short-term interest rates as soon as inflation has gone down a bit. In the disinflationary phase, the downward course of interest rates follows the downward trend of inflation. Even when nominal interest rates go down, the real interest rates remain positive and may even rise.

Here we have another example of a lag between the level of inflation and the level of interest rates. This time, disinflation is the front-runner and interest rates are following with a delay, exactly the opposite as in the preceding phase of the inflationary upswing.

In the beginning stage of the third phase of the long waves, the stimulating effect on the Y-component of the economy is rather weak. The X-component, on the other hand, expands immediately. The stock and bond market and the real estate market show strong gains. The upswing at the financial markets is especially noticeable, because the assets traded at the stock market and the bond market can be turned over so quickly. It can be said that the beginning of the disinflationary upswing is above all shaped by the financial markets.

Lower nominal interest rates have the effect that the relative value of stock dividends are rising compared to the return of bank deposits. If the saver has a return of 10 percent, there is no reason to buy stocks which provide a return of 10 percent at its current price. But if interest rates for his deposits are lowered to 9 percent, stocks with a dividend of 10 percent suddenly become attractive.

The reduced costs of financing the purchase of stocks make them more attractive too. In the United States, it is the custom to buy stocks "on margin." The stocks are used as "security" for a bank credit, which covers a large percentage of the current value of the purchased stock. Each dollar of the speculator's own money thus gets a lot of leverage. With only a small stake, the investor can make use of large amounts of funds for his speculation, which multiplies the payoff—or the loss.

The U.S. stock markets are therefore tightly connected with banks. Rising stock prices increase the value of the pledged security, permitting the speculator to obtain more credit to purchase more stocks. As the value of stocks increases, the credit volume expands.

Since stocks are old assets and are part of the X-component, their increase in value does not affect the Y-component directly very much. Of course, the profits and losses become part of the gross national product, but no bricks and mortars are used, no labor is involved. The good thing is that there is no direct inflationary effect, and only when the lucky speculators spend part of their riches for luxury automobiles and mansions is the Y-component visibly stimulated.

With real estate, it's a different matter. The sale of old houses by itself is a transaction within the X-component. The same as with stocks, only the realized profits and losses become part of the Y-component. But increasing prices of old houses, beneficial as they may be to the sellers, have a negative impact as well as they drive up the cost of housing. A booming real estate market has a substantial inflationary impact as rents adjust to the higher price level of owned houses and condos. But in America, this side of a real estate boom is mostly overlooked as the inflationary impact of the real estate boom is more than compensated by the moderating prices of other goods.

In this phase, all the attention is focused on the wonderful effects of rising real estate prices. Anybody who qualifies for a mortgage has a chance to get wealthy. Home-equity loans make life so much nicer.

And do not forget all the new construction which is taking place, because it has become so profitable. All kinds of tradesmen are in demand and fetch good wages. Plumbers are paid as well as heart surgeons.

The boom in stocks and real estate continues as long as inflation, measured by yardsticks like the consumer price index or the cost living index, goes down. Why is that so? The reason is that the banks are now financing the increase in stock and real estate prices. You may consider the price run-up of these items as another form of "inflation." But since the "strength" of the stock market and the real estate market are viewed as benign, the disinflationary upswing continues. It is thus the changed direction of bank credit which shapes the third phase of the long waves.

Since new money is channeled through the speculation into the economy, the X-Component expands while the Y-component stagnates in the beginning. Those who do not participate at the speculation can watch the nouveau riche build their mansions at the most desirable locations, buy yachts and private airplanes and other luxury items. Firms who cater to the luxury market prosper, while the mass market stays weak for some time.

It is not without irony that it is the spending of the newly rich which finally let the Y-component grow. Its expansion begins when the lucky speculators use their new wealth for living expenses. Soon the middle class cashes in on the risen value of their homes by getting home-equity loans.

While the great master John Maynard Keynes assumed that banks use the money entrusted to them to finance investments, the reality is different. They finance speculators as well, and they provide credit for the purchase of consumer goods.

The credit card may even be considered the symbol of the modern way of life. Through the eyes of Keynes, the effect of consumer credit cannot be calculated because the master only considers net savings. At the basis of our Ping-Pong model, we have no trouble observing the path of money provided by credit cards and other forms of consumer credit, although this kind of spending does not fit perfectly into our concept of economic development under the rule of central bank money.

After all, our theory of the long waves is based on the assumption that banks give loans mostly to finance projects deemed profitable, which have a high likelihood of a steady stream of interest payments and eventual repayment of the loan. Consumer loans have no "productive" purpose, and their repayment is doubtful. Therefore, these loans are often frowned upon.

Cultural critics consider these loans as a sign of irresponsibility, maybe even cultural decline. That may be true. There is no doubt that accumulated credit card debt can become a financial and psychological burden for the indebted people, who may almost feel enslaved by the banks.

It certainly would be much better if the people had enough income to pay their living expenses instead of borrowing the funds to create the lifestyle desired.

But the truth is that these consumer loans are very beneficial to the economy within the framework of a monetary system based on central bank money. This is especially true during the third phase of the long waves. These loans do not finance any speculation, trigger the production of additional goods and services, and directly strengthen the Y-component of the economy.

The credit-financed expenses do not determine the character of this phase, but they help to lengthen it by getting the production of goods going and creating jobs and income.

Credit cards add to the dynamic of the economy since the banks do not measure the credit-worthiness by proof of income but by people's record in paying interest rates on time.

You may have little income, but as long as you meet your financial obligation, you are a good credit risk. I think this is quite a "progressive" element of today's monetary system.

In the phase of the disinflationary upswing, the credit card business is very profitable for the lenders because the slide of interest rates charged by the central bank lowers the banks' costs of refinancing. Therefore, the banks are pushing for credit card loans, and by doing so, they strengthen the Y-component.

While the beginning of the third phase is very characterized by the booming stock market, later on it is real estate which attracts more and more people. At the end of this phase, the whole nation is speculating in houses. The boom in real estate is slow at the beginning because the memory of the bust at the end of the inflationary upswing lingers on. Also, since the inflation is easing, there is no flight from money into concrete.

On the other hand, lower interest rates make houses more affordable—and lift their prices. Also, homeowners profit from lower interest rates as they can refinance their existing mortgages, which frees part of their income which they can use for consumption or other purposes. This strengthens the Y-component of the economy.

The second mortgages have same effect, which gives homeowners the chance to tap into the increased equity of their house.

The real estate boom soon becomes the main pillar of the economic expansion, strengthening the X-component and the Y-component alike. The growing national product creates sound profits, which encourage institutional and private investors to buy more stocks, pushing up their prices. The effective yield may be low as speculators anticipate further gains in stock prices. Eventually, there comes the moment when the stock prices lose touch with the existing realities.

The same thing happens with real estate. The population becomes convinced that buying real estate is the proven way to become rich quickly. Others jump on the bandwagon because they are afraid that otherwise they will never again have the chance of owning a house. Society seems to be split in a class of wealthy real estate owners and poor renters. Even when the expensive houses can only be rented at a loss, the frenzy continues.

It is quite possible that the upswing is interrupted for a while, when the central bank doesn't lower interest rates as needed for the party to continue. It's conceivable, although not rational, that the central bank even raises interest rates during that phase of the long waves. That's what the Federal Reserve did in the summer of 1987. It was never thoroughly explained why Mr. Greenspan did this. It may have been an attempt to reduce the trade deficit of the United States by slowing down the economy. The following crash demonstrated how little our monetary policymakers understand the workings of the economy based on central bank money.

Luckily, the damage of such a crash in the middle of the disinflationary upswing is limited if the central bank reverses its course and lowers the interest rates once again. At this stage of the third phase, the level of interest rates is high enough to permit a rate decrease substantial enough to stimulate lending for purchasing securities. For that reason, the stock market can recover rather quickly and not much harm is done by this accident.

It becomes a totally different story as soon as the disinflationary upswing approaches the turning point where inflation and interest rates have reached zero percent.

Tragically, it is in this last stretch of the third phase, when speculators in stocks and real estate go wild because credit is so cheap and the rewards of ever-increasing stock and real estate prices are so tempting, that very few speculators can resist the urge.

But because interest rates are so low, the central bank has lost its capacity to stimulate the economy. It cannot lower the cost of borrowing any further. The value of stocks and real estate compared to deposits of money does not rise anymore.

Under these circumstances, the crash of the stock market and the collapse of the real estate market are unavoidable. This marks the end of the disinflationary upswing.

Chapter 7

Crash and Depression

All prophets of gloom and doom face the same question: "When will it happen?" The smart ones avoid giving a precise date. But there are always some prophets who claim to know exactly when the calamity will occur. One of those is Dr. Ravo Batra, who in 1985 published a book under the title *The Great Depression of 1990*. The book became a best seller, and the crash of 1987 appeared to be a confirmation of his prediction. But since the year 1990 went by without the world economy getting depressed, Batra's warnings appeared baseless. But I think the good doctor showed at least good instincts about the fragile nature of the economy. I found some useful facts in his books, besides some mumbo jumbo. I do not think, though, that he developed a rational theory of the long waves. But I appreciate that he had come to the conclusion that the mainstream economics did not grasp the very nature of the problem.

I had predicted the stock market crash of 1987, and when it happened, I was stunned by the accuracy of my own prediction. But I knew that this crash was not the one which precedes the depression. The conditions were not ripe yet. I feel that at the turn of the century—in ten years—America's and the whole world's economy will be at the verge of a terrible economic contraction. My capabilities as a clairvoyant are not good enough, though, to make a precise prediction. But I am betting your money on the year 2000. It has a round number, and that is already useful as a measuring pole for the time frame to place the big D.

Please, don't think that if this year will pass by without the occurrence of an economic earthquake, that the dangers have disappeared. The crisis will come soon enough. Of course, it is possible that the politicians until then will have taken some measures which will stretch the third phase of the long waves and postpone the beginning of the depression for a few years.

More important than predicting the precise time of the beginning depression is to make the public aware of the constellation of economic conditions which make the disinflationary upswing turn into a depression. I would warn to wait for the big crash of the stock market like in 1929, although I did include such a crash in the ideal-typical course of the long waves. Each long-term cycle has many similarities, but each one is different. For example, it is possible that the overspeculation at the end of the third phase occurs years before the described critical point. So the precipice at the very end of the phase may not be all that steep. Also, it may well be that the most spectacular development at the end of the third phase could be the collapse of the real estate boom and not the crash of the stock market.

It would be wrong to think that it is the impact of the falling stocks and house prices which causes the depression. The cause is the lacking ability of the banks to find profitable projects to fund loans. The preceding inflation as well as the following disinflation offered plenty of opportunities to lend. These opportunities are gone now.

In order to determine the critical point where disinflation turns into deflation and the boom turns into bust, it helps to get an understanding of the forces which shape the development of interest for central bank credit. For the sake of simplicity, we used Schumpeter's method and consolidated data of inflation and

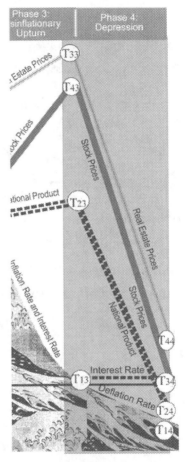

Diagram 18

Starting at turning point T13, interest rates and inflation are not locked anymore. When the inflation rate has fallen to zero percent, interest rates cannot drop any further.

As disinflation turns into deflation, the gap between interest rates and the changing price index widens and real interest rates are rising. Because of this disconnect between falling prices and nominal interest rates, the depression accelerates.

interest into one curve. Now the time has come to observe both data separately.

Regarding the development of interest rates, we take into account of the two main factors involved:

* The scarcity of capital and
* The compensation for economic misdirection, which is reflected in the prevailing inflation or deflation

There is also the delay of interest adjustment to be reckoned with. What we mean is the time lag between the first sign of economic misdirection and its reflection in the level of interest rates.

During the course of the long waves the real scarcity of capital is highest during its first period. It is declining over time because

* the demand for credit used for productive purposes weakens as saturation spreads and the demand for some goods is stagnating and
* the deposits in the bank accounts are increasing because of increased savings.

To which extent the real capital scarcity contributes to the development of interest rates can be illustrated as a line which goes down from a high level to zero. At the same time, the compensation for economic misdirection rises from the bottom to the level reflecting the peak of interest rates and then slides back to zero. This is easy to understand:

During the first phase of the long waves, the real scarcity of capital is high. But since there is no inflation, the level of interest rates is only affected by the scarcity of capital. The scarcity factor keeps interest rates well above the level of interest rates. When inflation pops up, interest rates start to rise, although the scarcity of capital continues to declines. But there is a time lag between the emerging signs of inflation and the interest rate adjustment. This delay is typical for the inflationary upswing. Without the delay, the economy would falter and the upturn would be put in hold or aborted.

During the disinflationary phase, the real scarcity of capital goes down further. The compensation for economic misdirection starts at a record level but recedes over the coming years. Again there is a time lag because the central bank waits for proof that the inflation rate has gone down another step. Without this delay, the long waves could enter another inflationary stretch.

We assume that the central bank will continue to follow this course and react with a certain delay to the next steps of disinflation.

Now what happens when inflation reaches zero percent? The compensation for economic misdirection should be zero. There is no scarcity of capita. Therefore, interest rates should be zero as well. But because of the delay of adjustment, interest rates may hover at a little higher rate, perhaps at 1 to 2 percent.

So the central banker may think that they still have some powder left. But actually it may be too little in order to counteract the effects of a crash of the stock market and/or the collapse of the real estate boom.

It could be argued that in the twenties the Federal Reserve kept interest rates too high. But even if the central bankers had adjusted the level of interest rates quicker to the lowered level of the price index, it wouldn't have made much of difference. Maybe it would have lengthened the third phase a little bit.

Now let us look at the current situation. (I am updating the original text of this treatise.) The federal funds rate is currently (in the year 2002) at 1.5 percent while the inflation oscillates between 2 and 3 percent.

So it seems there is no delay of adjustment. In the contrary, the level of interest rates is lower than the inflation rates. It seems to me that the Federal Reserve under the leadership of Alan Greenspan is trying to reinflate the economy and thus avoid the depression. The question is where this road leads and whether the public accepts the comeback of inflation.

If the central bank at some point in time decides to rein in the newly unleashed inflation, it may be hailed as virtuous, but the economy will resume the regular path of the third phase and will soon get close to the critical turning point as the central bank loses its ability to stimulate the economy any further.

It could be argued that the central bank could drive down borrowing costs even further by "charging" negative interest, practically rewarding the speculators for their good deeds. But I doubt that this will keep the economy from going downhill.

Now we have to have a look at the interest the member banks charge their customers. Of course, the prime rate for the bank's best customers is higher than the discount rate of the Federal Reserve. No surprise there. The banks want to make a profit and add a certain margin to the costs of funds. During most of the third phase, the prime rate follows the downward path of the federal funds rate. How much the margins over the borrowing costs of the banks are depends on many factors, including the degree of competition within the banking sector and the perceived riskiness of the loans.

Because of the risk factor, the prime rate doesn't go down anymore even though the central bank credit gets cheaper all the time. This is easy to understand. If the economy gets shaky and the prices of houses tumble down, the banks must try to cover the increased risks by charging higher interest rates. This is the other reason why monetary policy alone is not sufficient to prevent a plunge into the depression.

I think it is not necessary to describe the calamity which such a depression would inflict on America and the whole world economy. The numbers of people alive who experienced the Depression in the thirties may be dwindling. But their offspring know from stories told, from books and movies how much despair and suffering such a massive economic crisis inflicts upon the people. It is the first priority of all politicians to take the right steps to prevent a depression.

For a while politicians felt confident that they could preclude such a crisis by the Keynesian deficit spending. Didn't Richard Nixon say that "we are all Keynesian now"?

But Keynesian remedies have proven to be a blessing with serious side effects: a bloated government, widening budget deficits which lead to higher taxes. The current U.S. deficit is already so huge that the thought of more deficit spending appears almost as frivolous.

It seems we are trapped. The reader of this treatise will understand soon how we can be free from this trap. It's all a matter of the mind.

Chapter 8

The Empowerment of the Mint

What can be done to save us from the depression? I think the answers can be found in our narrative, how the sturdy original economy was transformed into the fragile one which goes through expansion, inflation, and disinflation until it reaches the point where the abyss of the depression looms. To pinpoint the causes of this pattern, we have to remind ourselves of the fundamental truth that the economic process starts with the production of money. In the original economy, the production of gold coins creates incomes which get the economy going, until all gold coins are retired. As long as the miners and minters are able to keep up the production of coins at the same level, the economy remains stable. All these change when the banks get involved and begin to recycle the money and start to create their own money, which enters the economy in the form of credit. Most of it is recycled and not retired.

It is the change in the quality of money, brought about by the banks, which is the main cause of the instability of today's economy.

Can the genie be put back in the bottle again, at least partially? I think it can and it must. The first step into this direction is to debunk the myth that today's monetary system is God-given and cannot be changed. It can be changed, but the resistance to change will be formidable. It could be said that there is a conspiracy at work. The conspirators are all of us, because all of us think that we are profiting from this system. We found the enemy, and the enemy was us.

Of course, we all are much too gullible and are prone to believe in myths and other propaganda without checking the facts. The assertion that the banks must be in charge of the creation of money is such a myth. It reminds me of the belief that babies are brought into this world by the *Klapperstorch*, as the Germans call the stork in children's lingo. Did you know that the stork not only brings us the babies but the newborn money as well? I have to admit that no financial expert has ever made this claim. But they come close to it when they make us believe that the new money is made "out of thin air" by the banks. Thin air—isn't that the realm of the stork?

Maybe Adebar the stork is not directly involved. But we know for sure that we are dealing with a kind of fairy tale when even the experts tell us that the bank finds the new money in their offices. Or let us put it more bluntly, we are confronted with an outright lie. But we don't want to admit it, because everybody else firmly believes in this tale.

It is noteworthy that this new money supposedly has no owner. The banks don't claim to own it. They claim to be just the finder who use it for their lending and, thus, for the benefit of all of us. But in a capitalist economy, everything is about ownership. Capitalists would like to parcel the sky and sell it to the highest bidder. So why does the new money have no owner?

The answer is this: because somebody else is the real owner. Some institution which remains in the dark and is never mentioned

Our search for the origin of today's money has revealed that the central bank actually is only a transit station for the distribution of newly created money. The balance sheet of the central bank shows that the new money is borrowed from an undisclosed source. When the central bank provides credit to their member banks, this act results in the following entries in its balance sheet: claims (against the member banks) and debt of the same amount to Unknown.

Who is the debtor? Nobody knows, and nobody wants to know. The bookkeeping trail of this money appears to be lost.

But it isn't. All the evidence proves that the trail leads to the mint. The mint is the institution of the sovereign state which used to coin the money in the old days when it was made out of gold, silver, or other precious metals. Actually, the mint still owns the new money, even though the mint currently produces mostly coins used for change. The mint may have granted the banks the license to produce the larger amounts of money by issuing banknotes and by entries in their own ledger. But the ownership of all that newly created money remains with the mint. That's why the banks should pay interest to the mint. Only then can they rightfully charge interest themselves. (If the money would have been found, they wouldn't have the right to demand interest. But perhaps the banks consider the interest they extract from their customers as kind of a finder's fee.)

It does not take much to reestablish the old role of the mint which has been obscured by the banking sector, which over the centuries has wrested away the control of the money from the mint by demonetizing it via issuing credit and printing banknotes. Congress gave the mint the responsibility for the coinage of all money. By this, Congress made it crystal clear that money is not just a veil over the economic transaction and that it is not identical with credit either. Money is a product whose ingredients were very expensive once. Because of the high material cost of the gold coins, the mint used to make only a modest profit—just a compensation for its service of weighing and grading the metal and turning it into coins. Today's money is made out of paper or is created as an entry in a computerized account. The production costs are negligible. Therefore, the mint makes a profit which almost equals the nominal value of the created money.

It is today's hidden practice that the mint lends all its produced money to the central bank. Lifting the secret of the mint's role in the production and distribution of new money does not mean that the established practice has to be changed.

The mint may continue to lend all its produced money to the central bank if this practice is best for the whole economy.

But acknowledging the central bank's dependence on the mint (and its obligation to pay interest on it) would be the first step in the direction of making the dollar as sound as gold.

When this relationship is established, the mint can use part of the money it produces for other purposes. After all, 99.9 percent of the produced monies are pure profit. The mint can use this profit by distributing it to the people. This could be in the form of direct payments to taxpayers or as lump sums to the government, which distributes the funds. It could be used for government expenditures or as a means to cover deficits of the federal government's budget.

As the result of such an empowerment of the mint, the monetary system would become similar to that of a system based on gold. As we have learned earlier, when gold coins serve as currency and no banks exist, newly found money is injected as income (of the miners and minters), and after it has taken its path through the economy, it is retired. If the mint distributes at least part of its produced money in this old-fashioned way and creates net incomes of people, the quality of the monetary system has already changed. The money starts to behave more like money made out of gold. mint money turns into "paper-gold" when it is not recycled but retired. The economy begins to stabilize.

Now the question arises: how much money can the mint produce, and how much should it provide for the banks, and how much should be distributed as income? So the mint has to come to grips not only with the questions, which the central bank routinely has to answer today, but it must make a determination on how much additional income it must distribute in order to keep the economy growing, without igniting inflation.

It was said by some astute observer that the best chairmen of the Federal Reserve made their decisions "by the seat of their pants." I guess that would be true as well for the individuals who decide the policy of the mint. Several factors must be considered. One is the degree of utilization of the economy. If unemployment is high and the production facilities are underused, the income policy of the mint could be more expansive than if unemployment is low. Another factor is the amount people save without letting the bank use the funds for loans.

A system of paper-gold can only function if policymakers make a rational decision about the amount of new money to be created and about the direction of it. The right mix of credit expansion and income distribution must be found in order to reach the goal of zero inflation and full employment. Like in life in general, the right proportions are the key to success.

The built-in capacity for a rational money and income policy is a feature of paper-gold, which sets it apart from a monetary system based on gold coins, whose money supply is determined by the unpredictable output of the mines. Since the mines usually cannot expand the production of precious metal by leaps and bounds, the supply of coins may be quite stable most of the time. This fact is considered to be the safeguard against inflation.

But the truth is that the gold production is not stable at all. During long periods there had been shortages of gold, and the economy suffered from it. There had been periods of abundance as well, but most of the time it was in short supply—why almost everybody accepted the banknotes as supplemental money which in the end totally replaced the gold coins.

Another feature of paper-gold compared to gold coins is the wide range of the income policies which it permits. The "income policy" which the production of gold coins entailed consisted of providing profit to the operators of the mines and to the landowners who permitted the operation of the mine. It gave income to the miners and to all parties involved in the coinage of the metal, including the sovereign who guaranteed the quantity and the quality of the metal by stamping his seal on each piece of it.

With paper-gold the range of people who can directly profit from the production of money is much wider than with gold coins. Actually, the mint can distribute the money to anybody, as long as this is consistent with reaching the goal of zero inflation and zero unemployment. The mint may choose to fund government expenses as well. Actually, the mint could pay for all budget deficits of the central government, making it unnecessary to borrow.

At the end of the disinflationary phase, the shortcomings of the central bank money begin to have the most devastating effect because the credit machine slows down dramatically. In this situation, continuing injections of money in the form of income are enormously beneficial. The mint can help!

Since the mint uses its own profits for these transfers, it does not have to make loans for this purpose. It can distribute these monies like presents. The result is an increase in net incomes without amassing any debt. As there is no additional debt to worry about, no future tax increases must be taken in consideration. The amount of money at the mint's disposal would be rather small if it would only consist of the funds which the central bank lends to its member banks. But it is important to understand why the member banks borrow so little from the central bank compared to the total volume of credit which they provide to their customers. The reason is that the member banks hold only few reserves because each piece of money is used simultaneously many times over. This is comparable to the absurd situation where a loaf of bread is eaten at the same time by a multitude of people.

If the banks are required to increase their reserves, they must borrow more from the central bank if they want to keep their lending at the current level.

Let us assume that the banks were required to hold 50 percent of their credit volume as reserves. This would mean that each dollar deposited would be used twice simultaneously: the same dollar saved is used at the same time for a loan. If the bank funds a project which fails, the same amount of deposited money would be lost but the rest of the deposits would still be safe. This is quite an improvement compared to today's banking practice.

Today only a small fraction of deposits are used as reserves, and each dollar is used simultaneously much more often. Any failed loan wipes out a much larger portion of the deposits, and all too often, the losses exceed the total reserves. Hence depositing money at a bank is a risky proposition, especially if you deposit in larger than the amount covered by the Federal Deposit Insurance. The bank crisis which occurs at the end of the third phase of the long waves can even topple the FDIC.

Any increase in required reserves not only improves the safety of the deposited money, but also enlarges the pool of retired money which is not recycled by the banks. The more money is retired, the more new money can be created by the mint.

At the disposal of the mint is not only the amount equal to the retired savings. A growing economy needs additional funds. If the economy is underutilized, the mint can channel more money into the economy by income policy. Even if the slack is gone, a growing economy needs more money to facilitate the increased output. The mint may decide to use more money for loans to the central bank, or it may decide to distribute more income.

All this may appear like a total break with the current practices. But it is not a revolution which I am calling for, it is an evolution which can be accomplished without great upheavals. Actually, all the institutions involved in a system of minted money already exist. They would only play different roles. The mint would assume the responsibility for monetary policy, which now the central bank has. Its dual role as a governmental agency and a bank would be ended. The Federal Reserve would become just a bank.

Contrary to today's central bank, the mint can provide credit to the banks, provide subsidies to the government or income to the public. I am sure some experts consider this a strange and possibly dangerous mix of monetary and fiscal policy. But there is no denying that originally the production of golden money had a "fiscal" dimension, as miners and minters received incomes. It would be wrong to deny the mint such a fiscal role just for the sake of adhering to the purity of the categories "monetary" policy and "fiscal" policy.

It is true that the powers of the mint could be abused. It is conceivable that people in charge of the mint could be corrupted and would steer monies into the pockets of some cronies. Therefore, there must be total transparency in the decision making of the mint. Of course, the mint must formulate its policies in consultation with the Federal Reserve and those institutions which shape fiscal policy. The mint could be part of either the executive or it could be an independent body whose policies are determined by some wise men and women.

As soon as the empowerment of the mint has taken place, the turning point at the end of the third phase has lost much of its horror. True, when interest rates have reached zero percent, the central bank has lost its capacity to stabilize the economy by further interest rate cuts, and the value of other assets, relative to treasury bills, doesn't increase automatically anymore. There is no room for more speculation in these assets, and capital investments come to a standstill. The X-component and the Y-component are paralyzed.

This is the moment when the mint must act. By feeding additional income into the economy, the crisis can be averted.

Actually, this is a moment which asks for some sort of celebration. After all, inflation has been demolished. When the mint is empowered and its powers are used wisely, there is no reason to be afraid when deflation sets in and that the economy begins to spiral into a depression. Not only can the mint shield us from such a depression, but it can also pave the way for a long-lasting phase of prosperity without inflation.

Suddenly the debt of the U.S. government doesn't loom over so largely anymore. Because when the discount rate of the central bank falls to zero, long-term interest rates follow suit, when the bond market anticipates enduring stability of the price index. If that anticipation proves to be true, the price of treasury bonds and bills will go up and their effective rate will approach zero percent as well. When this happens, the difference between pieces of money and pieces of federal debt mostly evaporates. Both papers carry no interest. At this moment, the truth is revealed that treasury bonds and bills may constitute "debt" in legal terms but not in economic terms. Economically these papers are instruments of true savings—retired money.

Now it may be argued that interest rates will not stay that low for long. Everybody knows from experience that interest rates never stay at the same level. But our experience is tied to a monetary system based on central bank money, which creates the phases of the long waves.

But in a system based on minted money, the price index can be stabilized. Inflation can stay zero for good. While the functioning of the economy with central bank money at certain stages requires inflation and then disinflation, minted money is capable of price stability. Actually, it requires price stability if it shall assume the quality of money made out of gold. mint money turns into 100 percent "paper-gold" when all newly created money is introduced into the economy in the form of income and all savings are retired.

Under these conditions, banks would depend totally on their borrowing from the mint. All the deposits would be totally safe. The mint would ultimately assume all the risks the banks are taking by lending money.

Not that I would favor such an extreme system. I mention it only as a yardstick for our thinking. Possibly a workable solution could be to distribute all minted money to individuals, who would continue to deposit their money on bank accounts. If the banks can use part of their money for issuing loans, they could operate without having access to mint credit.

As often, the best solution lies in the middle. I now think the best system would be a mixed one, like today, and give the banks access to mint credit and let them use part of the deposits of savers for their lending. The mint then would have to decide how much money it should lend to the central bank, which parcels out the funds by providing credit to its member banks.

So there are many possibilities to create a mixed system which provides more stability and more growth. The minted money could consist only of 10 percent paper-gold and still provide a backbone for the economy, which permits continuity in growth and stable prices. It is up to the policymakers to find the right mixture of newly minted paper money and paper-gold. All policies must serve the goal to keep the inflation rate at zero percent. With central bank money, this goal can only be achieved by austerity, by trading off employment and price stability. minted money, on the other hand, permits a forward strategy because the mint has two tools to work with: it can provide credit and it can provide income. If it uses its power wisely, there will be opportunities for capital investments once again and the banks can finance the growth of the real economy instead of financing speculation and fostering asset inflation. With minted money at their disposal, policymakers have the means to combat the ugly siblings of inflation and unemployment at the same time.

Chapter 9
Mint Policies

In all phases of the long waves, the mint can help to steady the economic development because it can provide credit as well as income. The executioner of its credit policy would be the central bank. The mint would allot a certain amount of money for the credit to the central bank, which would extend the credit to its member banks. The most practical way to portion the money would be that the mint sets interest rates to the central bank. So the credit policy would be conducted by the mint in consultation with the central bank. For that purpose, the policymaking bodies of today's central bank should be moved under the roof of the mint providing continuity and skills. That would be a rather simple reorganization.

How to exert the power of providing income is a trickier question because the mint may become a rival of the government institutions who are participants in the budget process. I think there are two solutions to choose from.

The first solution would be that the Congress votes on the government's budget proposals as it does now and the mint automatically provides the money to cover any deficits. If the mint comes to the conclusion that the state of the economy warrants the distribution of additional income, the wise men and women at the helm of the mint could do so. This would leave the current power structure as it is.

The other solution would be committing Congress to balance the budget and leave it to the mint to stimulate the economy by dispensing income to people or funding projects which make the economy stronger.

Whatever method is chosen, policymakers now are in a much better position to even out the long waves of economic development and to make prosperity reach everybody.

During the first phase of long waves, the mint can be content in providing the credit which the central bank requests. This is the phase where the perfect Keynesian game is played: credit is mostly used to finance capital investments which create chains of income and savings, which in turn are used to finance more investments and make the economy grow vigorously.

At the beginning of the second phase of the long waves, the mint is called into action as soon as the economy is stuttering when demand for some products is slowing down. This may be the case because the demand has been saturated. Most likely, though, the demand has slowed down because of increased savings and because the distribution of income is such that the recipients of lower incomes cannot afford the products which the producers are trying to sell. The mint therefore has a good chance of averting the severe recession, which marks the onset of the second phase of the long waves.

The mint can do the trick if it chooses the right policy mix: providing additional incomes but keeping interest rates relatively high. This way, the Y-component is strengthened. Because of the additional income-financed demand, it makes sense for the producers to expand their production capacities, providing banks the chance to make more loans to participants of the Y-component. The relatively firm interest rates, on the other hand, discourage people to speculate in real estate and other assets. Therefore, the action of the mint emanates two different anti-inflationary effects. It keeps the prices of assets under wraps, and it helps producers reap all the benefits of the economies of scale due to increased mass production.

How should be the level of interest rates? It should be higher than inflation. The real interest rates should be positive.

I certainly would not declare that the mint could prolong the first phase of the long wave forever. Eternal prosperity exists only in paradise. There are always obstacles against the return to it. The disturbances might come from very different sources. Still, I think it should be possible to avoid the inflationary spiral which later on turns into the disinflationary upswing, which leads to the depression.

The third phase of the long waves can either stretch over two decades or be very short.

Assuming that the politicians have let the inflation spiral to a level at which it starts to feed itself and begins to destroy the fabric of the economy, the mint has basically two options. It can choose a radical approach or a gradual approach.

The radical approach would be if policymakers attempt to eradicate inflation quickly. This would mean that interest rates would be jacked up as long as it takes to stop most speculation and wipe out inflation.

As soon as inflation reaches zero percent, interest rates could be lowered dramatically. This would not reignite inflation as long as the inflation rate is lower than the level of interest rates. But as soon as inflation rates are getting closer to zero percent, the conventional monetary policy wouldn't allow stopping the contraction of the economy. The disinflationary phase would be very short. The radical approach would hasten the plunge into the depression.

But before this happens, the mint could use its power and unleash a surge of income by dispensing funds to the people who would gladly spend the money and let the economy jump over the depression right into a new first phase of recovery and expansion.

Such a daredevil strategy would need a very astute steering of the economy by the mint. Whether such a precise management of the economy is even possible, I don't know.

The gradual approach, which would force down inflations slowly but surely, seems to be more realistic.

As soon as inflation recedes a little bit and interest rates follow suit, the market value of stocks, real estate, and other assets rises, which may be wonderful for the speculators, but this creates huge problems for the whole of the economy. How high the asset inflation will go and how long the boom lasts depends on the height of inflation at the turning point from phase 2 to phase 3. If the peak of inflation was 10 percent, the length of the disinflationary upswing will be much longer and the increase in stock and real estate prices will be much higher than if the peak of inflation was only 5 percent.

I doubt that the mint can prevent the inflation of assets. It may try to establish a dual system of credit, charging higher rates for loans financing speculation and lower rates for capital investments. Whether that is feasible, I do not know. It may screw up the whole banking system.

But the mint may manage to lengthen the phase of the disinflationary upswing by using the tool of income policies. The necessity to do so may not be obvious to policymakers, and since a continuing easing of inflation rates must be a desirable outcome of its policies, the consequence of sliding interest rates cannot be avoided. Under these circumstances the economy will be going in the direction of the abyss.

The mint may be able to put a damper on the exuberance of the speculation by keeping interest rates relatively high while feeding an additional stream of incomes into the economy. This way, the mint may keep the prices of assets from reaching absurd heights and therefore limit the impact of the following fall. Only when the mint is fully aware of the dangers and takes vigorous countermeasures can the crash of the stock market and the collapse of the real estate market be averted, when the interest level approaches zero percent.

At the beginning of the fourth phase of the long waves, the mint must counteract.

When stocks have crashed and many houses are worth less than the amount of the mortgage, the mint can help keep the economy from falling into the depression and instead lay the groundwork for a long-lasting prosperity.

Policymakers must deal with a situation where huge chunks of the bank's assets will be wiped out, and many banks are facing the dreaded truth that the market value of the pawned stocks and real estate don't cover the total amount of issued credit. Since this affects the whole banking sector, the Federal Deposit Insurance doesn't have enough funds to secure all deposits. A run on the banks would bring about a total collapse of the banking sector if the government does not intervene. Huge amounts of money are needed to keep the bank in business. The mint could provide all the funds necessary either in the form of credit or as capital, which would give it the ownership of the banks.

Should the mint come to the rescue or not? Principled adherents to the concept of free markets will argue against it. After all, it's only fair that the banks take the consequences of their folly. Let new life emerge out of the ruins of the past. Schumpeter quotations will be heard frequently.

But what happens to the deposits of the bank's customers? If they exceed the limits set by the Federal Deposit Insurance, they would be lost anyway. Too bad.

The collapse of the banks and the destruction of deposits would do damage to the economy like of an earthquake of the magnitude measured by the top of the Richter scale. But let's not forget that this catastrophe has a positive side too. The "purpose" of the crash is, after all, to clean the slate, render harmless the excessive pools of money which distort the economy because they are used for speculation. By impoverishing people, it forces them to sell their assets cheaply, providing new opportunities to entrepreneurs and getting cash for their living expenses. This expands the Y-component and strengthens the economy. The economy will recover slowly—eventually.

Well, I am convinced that this will not happen. I think the memories of the last Depression are not all lost. And the banks, even in their sorry state, are much too powerful to suffer this fate. The politicians, hungry for campaign contributions, know what Percy Sutton knew: the banks are the place where the money is.

So the mint will have no choice other than forestall the collapse of the banks. Should the mint loan them the needed funds or provide capital and take over the banking sector?

I favor a temporary takeover, not because I want to socialize the banking sector, but because the banks during this crucial time are not helpful in overcoming the crisis. Especially when they have to pay back the huge sums they received as loans, they must try to squeeze as much profit out of their customers as possible. They will not lower the interest rates of existing mortgages, they will put all kind of obstacles in the path of those who want to refinance. They want to return to business as usual.

If the mint calls the shots at most major banks, it can establish lending practices which will help people to keep their houses and stay solvent.

But as a realist, I can't see that happen. I think the banks will be kept afloat by loans. Even if the mint will be independent, it will not be able to get the banks under control, not even temporarily.

This means that the salvation will not come from the credit policy. It must come from the income policy of the mint.

How much is needed to get the economy going? Actually, that's the wrong question, because the mint does not have to reason how it can achieve the most bang for the buck. In this way of thinking, fiscals and Keynesians are united because they assume that the monies must be raised by incurring debt which must be paid back. But the mint does not have to borrow. The monies the mint is forwarding must not be paid back. The right question therefore is how much money can the mint pump into the economy without causing inflation.

Since the money which the mint distributes must not be paid back, the most destructive effects of Keynesian policies can be avoided. There is no need for future tax increases in order to reduce the debt load of the government. Therefore, there is no danger that the intervention of the mint brings stagnation or stagflation upon the economy.

So instead of finding a way to make the most of every dollar, the task at hand is to increase the welfare of the people as much as possible. Additional net income is a good thing if it helps to rebalance the distribution of income and it provides purchasing power to the middle class and to the working people, who have trouble meeting their living expenses.

The established way to diminish the disparity of income is to use the tool of taxation. Surely, taxation has its merits in order to level the playing field somewhat. Yes, some steep tax on the tremendous gains of the speculators would be heartening to the common folks. Actually, it would be wonderful if all billionaires would be asked to "please" give up half of their wealth. Warren Buffet would still live frugally. Most of the other billionaires could still live like kings. Ideally, the tax policies should be such that the offspring of the wealthy have to earn their own money. But alas! That is a difficult thing to achieve, and it might do more harm than good.

So instead of getting lost in the minefield of the tax code, I suggest that there is a different way to even out the worst discrepancies. Instead of letting the IRS take away a larger share of the income of "the rich," the mint can give some additional income to the poor and the middle class. How much money the mint can distribute depends on the effects which it has on the recipients. Financing the building of pyramids, as Keynes suggested, is not very high on my priority list. Providing funds to the government for the purchase of some unneeded fighter planes may rank at the bottom of that list. But although my militaristic inclinations are weak, I must admit that spending additional money on defense is a very effective way to distribute income and create employment.

In regard of the discussion "more government or less taxes," I belong to the camp which prefers cuts of those taxes which burden people most, especially people with low incomes and the middle class. But tax relief for companies must also be considered as well to keep them in business and foster employment. Some countries tax companies very little, and this way, they are able to lure them to their shores. To keep the jobs of these companies at home, the mint should provide funds to lower the effective rates for these companies, while the government should try to harmonize these rates to stop this race of giving favors to some of the most profitable companies on earth.

There are certainly some projects which deserve to be funded by the mint. But I reject the Keynesian notion that the expansive effect of direct government spending is quicker and stronger than tax cuts. It is difficult to get the building of pyramids and other infrastructure projects going. Building or repairing roads is a highly mechanized business which creates little employment.

Keynes's calculation, that the expansive effects of government expenditures is bigger than tax cuts, sounds logical. In reality the opposite is true, because the governmental institutions are not able to start building the next day.

Furthermore, Keynes's preference for governmental expenses is rooted in the notion that the funds allocated should offer "the most bang for the buck." Since Keynes assumes that deficits causes debts, he prefers government projects which require the lowest amount of funds and offer the biggest surge in growth and additional employment. From our point of view, these considerations are mostly irrelevant. In our view, tax cuts are no waste of money. If they are financed by the mint, the funds must not be paid back, and therefore, no additional taxes must be raised later on. Therefore, the choice of projects should be focused on their impact on the general welfare, not on their turbo effect on the expansion of the economy. The more taxes can be cut for this purpose without awakening the economy inflation, the better.

Unfortunately, the choosing is often influenced by special interests which steer the money to projects which can be considered "pork." Government projects tend to be overpriced as well, because they are often designed to satisfy the involved contractor's appetite for profits and the unions' desire for high wages. Ever since President John F. Kennedy, by executive order, permitted unions to organize the workforce of all federal institutions, the obstacles against padding their cushy positions at the expense of the taxpaying public have been severely weakened. In my view, today's American unions are not the benevolent organizations anymore which once battled against the abuse and injustice inflicted upon the workers. Especially the unions which represent government employees have secured salaries and benefits exceeding those of equivalent jobs in the private sector. Additional government expenditures must be suspected to be self-serving to the unions and their members. Therefore, I consider government expenditures as the least attractive way to channel minted money into the economy. But this option should not be ruled out if there are projects which are highly beneficial to all citizens.

When the mint assumes responsibility for conducting the monetary policy, policymakers are getting an efficient and painless tool for the task of making the income distribution more balanced. This should not be done only for the sake of some notion of justice, but for the sake of keeping the motor of the economy humming.

Within the political debate, tax cuts fostering consumption are often pitted against tax cuts which supposedly lead to more savings and more investment. But this reasoning is far too simplistic, because capital investments are usually undertaken when existing production capacities are used up. If a company has more than enough capacities to meet the current demand, it will not build another factory just because its owners' net income has been increased by a tax cut. But if the demand for its products rises, the company may have good reasons to do so.

Strengthening mass demand has the additional benefit, that it has a moderating influence on inflation. Of course, it is quite possible that an increase in demand for certain products creates shortages—Keynesian bottlenecks—which are pushing up prices. But the cyclical inflation we are mostly concerned with is the result of lacking demand, which increases productions costs per unit and which entices banks to channel more money into the X-component of the economy with inflationary side effects. For that reason, tax cuts which increase mass demand for pieces of the Y-component have anti-inflationary effects which permit even further tax cuts.

The usual method of income redistribution is the progressive income tax. I think a certain progression of the tax rates makes sense. But trying to squeeze more revenues out of the rich by making the tax more progressive usually requires a divisive struggle and may not accomplish too much. Tax cuts or even negative tax rates are the better method of providing more purchase power to the people of lower incomes.

Indeed, deficit-financed tax cuts can increase the net income of people, even when gross wages and salaries are stagnating. When money consisted of gold coins, its production enriched miners and minters. When the mint makes its money out of paper or per computer entry, we are all "miners and minters" who may get a share of the minting profit.

Therefore, the best tax cuts are those which reward all the people engaged in baking the big pie of the national product, encouraging people to hang in there, providing incentives to be more productive and innovative.

On top of the list of the possible taxes to be decimated are people's contributions to Social Security and to Medicare and the "payroll tax" which employers pay for funding Social Security. The payroll tax is an archaic tax anyhow, a residue of times when companies were responsible for the welfare of their employees, very much like the owners of cotton plantations who were once responsible for the "well being" of their slaves. The payroll tax burdens employees no less than the employees' own contributions to Social Security, because total labor cost determines whether a company can afford hiring people and it is the net pay which determines whether a job is worth taking.

A lighter tax load can improve the finances of people more than rising gross salaries since the increased gross pay is subject to additional taxation, possibly at a higher rate.

Lifting some of the burden of the Social Security tax and the payroll tax should be the first priority for the mint, because it will immediately reduce production costs. This has a direct anti-inflationary effect. In other words, the mint should help all us "miners and minters" to secure our retirement and help us in case of sickness. Such a policy frees part of the incomes to be spent on consumption without running up debt on people's credit cards.

There are certainly other taxes which impede economic growth. Taxing businesses more than they can bear is always a dangerous proposition, especially if those businesses can escape the taxes by relocating.

I am sure there are many more taxes which make good candidates for substitution by minted money. But let's not forget that the mint can have a positive effect on lending as well. When the economy reaches the brink of the depression, bankers are not the most popular people. But there is no reason to ready the guillotines because the bankers may not be personally guilty. Greed is the virtue which gets the market economy going. It is up to us, the people, to make sure that the greed results in a good outcome for the economy at large.

Of course, some bankers may deserve a spanking. But changing the monetary system and improving the lending practices is more important than punishing the misdeeds of some moneylender.

Without adjusting the lending practices of the banks, even the most aggressive income policy of the mint may not be enough to pull the economy back on the path to growth and prosperity.

One of the main features of the current system is the fact that the central bank only provides short-term loans to the member banks. The mortgage rates are therefore shaped by the capital markets, which take into account the long-term inflation expectation. It is, of course, quite natural that investors try to anticipate the future inflation and ask for compensation in form of higher rates if an increase in inflation seems to be likely. The understandable precaution of investors has the effect that mortgages remain much too high even when short-term rates have fallen to zero percent. Therefore, the banks provide no solution to the crisis.

As I mentioned before, I think that banks should be nationalized temporarily in order to provide credit, which helps to stabilize the real estate market and the economy at large. Another solution would be that the mint or the central bank automatically assumes existing mortgages and refinances them with low but flexible rates. This will cost the taxpayer nothing, since existing loans will be only replaced by other loans. Only the original debtors will be affected since their flow of high interest rates will cease. On the other hand, these capitalists would get back their money in full and would not have to suffer the losses due to the wave of foreclosures to be expected if the lending practices were not changed.

Now the mint would assume the risk of foreclosure. But if the interest rates charged to the owners of real estate would be lowered substantially, even houses bought at highly inflated prices would not be such a big burden anymore. Imagine interest rates of only 1 percent, and the whole picture would brighten. Theoretically, the mint could even charge an interest of zero percent. This might sound crazy in your ears. But you should take into account that your perception of the matter is conditioned by years of rising and then receding inflation. But when the mint takes over, continuing price stability should be its goal. This goal can be reached because the mint has credit policies and income policies at its disposal. In this environment, mortgages of zero percent are not as unrealistic as it seems.

Compared to the level of mortgages which would prevail if the normal lending practices of the banks would continue, any rate which the mint would charge would bring tremendous savings to the borrowers. These savings would provide a great boost to the economy. The low rates might not stop the slide of real estate prices if the housing stock had been expanded excessively during the boom years. But the low rates would help to reduce the drag of the real estate market on the economy.

It should not be the goal of the mint to push real estate prices up to their inflated level at the end of the disinflationary upswing. High real estate prices are not the sign of prosperity but an indicator of a misdirected bank loans. It should be the goal of policymakers to make housing affordable. When people have to allocate a large part of their income for housing, they are impoverished and must curtail their spending for bread and butter items and beautiful things which give them pleasure. All too often, people try to have the cake and eat it too by charging their credit cards.

Their credit card debt is the other millstone around the neck of most Americans. The mint has the power to erase that credit card debt. Such a measure, if this will ever be implemented, must be done with great caution, because people should not get the impression that they are rewarded for their folly. But there is no doubt that the banks have contributed to the huge debt load by flooding the country with their credit cards. This doesn't make the banks guilty of any crime because the banks only respond to the signals which the monetary policy is giving within the framework of a monetary system based on central bank money. If the banks cannot find takers for their credit, the economy falters. For that reason, the banks can claim that by expanding their portfolio of credit card debt they are able to keep the economy going.

So the responsibility for the huge credit card debt of Americans is not so much proof of lacking discipline or loose morality of the individuals, but proof of a misguided policy which depends too much on the ability of banks to inject loans into the economy and too little on its capacity to introduce new money in the form of additional income.

It would be only fair if an empowered mint would ameliorate the financial conditional conditions of Americans by lifting some of their credit card debt. Lack of available money may not the problem. Equitableness is. It cannot be that people with high credit card debt are rewarded while those who lived frugally are taken for granted.

An equitable way of debt relief would be that each taxpayer would get a certain sum with the mandate to pay off credit card debt. If the sum exceeds the debt of people, they could pocket the difference as an addition to their savings.

Whether this kind of action is really possible depends of the state of the economy and on the scope of other actions taken. As always, the size of the portions and their proportions to another matter. Too much stimulus may awaken an inflation of the Keynesian kind, where too much money chases too few goods and bottlenecks bring about price increases.

It should be noted, though, that this kind of inflation can be stopped in its tracks quite easily by other measures which would rein in too much demand for items of the Y-component. And please remember that higher production numbers increase the economies of scale, which results in lower costs per unit and reduces inflationary pressure. And don't forget that cyclical inflation is caused by too much credit and by a lack of income-financed demand.

If the relief of personal debt is measured carefully, there is no immediate, explosive surge of demand to be expected. But people can breathe easier, they feel liberated. And some of their income which they had tied up for paying interest on their credit card debt is now at their disposal for consumption. That's a thing at this critical stage of the long waves.

This means a lot for people who are afraid that they may be fired and whose equity in their house has dwindled. The money which was used to feed the banks now helps people make ends meet. Of course, the mint cannot be Santa Claus to all the people who recklessly misuse their credit cards. It is up to the banks, in conjunction with the government, to encourage people to live within their means.

Since the mint can do so much, the question must arise whether it can do something about the accumulated debt of the central government. The answer is yes, it can. Actually, the mint can wipe out the total debt. If the mint pays off the debt by purchasing treasuries, it takes ownership of these debt instruments. As the mint finances the purchase, not by credit bus but by spending part of its profit, the chain of credit stops right there. Since the mint is owned by the government, the government now owes billions of money to itself, which means the debt has been dissolved.

The former owners of the treasuries receive different kind of papers: money. How much money will suddenly flood the bank accounts? Not as much as you might think, because most of the treasuries were bought with central bank credit in the first place. The banks themselves own a big chunk of the treasuries. Private investors own huge amounts as well. When those investors bought these treasuries, their purchase reduced the amount of money in their bank accounts. The banks had to fill the gap by borrowing from the central bank. When these treasuries are now sold to the mint, the banks receive an influx of money, which enables them to reduce their borrowing from the central bank by the same amount.

With treasuries owned by foreign governments, the story is a little bit different. If the mint buys those treasuries (or does not issue new ones for expiring treasuries), those foreign governments will now hold money instead of debt papers. Receiving no interest may be disappointing. The governments may try other investments. Or for lack of better alternatives, they may just leave the money in their bank accounts.

While the debt of the government can easily be extinguished, this course of action doesn't rank at the top of my priority list. You see, if the mint pursues a sensible mix of credit and income policies, continuing price stability can be achieved. This means that the interest rates of treasuries is approaching zero percent. They may even become negative.

So why not give up the practice of issuing treasuries altogether and get rid of the bond market, where these papers are traded? Because the bond market helps to meet the other requirement of mint money: a substantial part of savings must not be recycled, but retired.

Indeed, the real purpose of government "debt" is not to finance governmental expenditures, but to provide a safe haven for monies laid back for rainy days. Treasuries are savings instruments. From the macroeconomic perspective, they constitute no debt.

Of course, savers could choose to keep their money in bank accounts. They might even get a little bit more interest for it than the return that treasuries can offer. But the savers may still prefer treasuries because they consider them safer, as banks can go bankrupt while the federal government never runs out of money (although some people are not so sure about that anymore). Keeping the market of federal bonds intact may make sense, even though the federal government does not need the funds to finance its expenses.

But on the other hand, a good argument can be made to stop issuing treasuries altogether. As long as the government issues bonds, people will be inclined to think that they constitute debt and that any increase of this debt is dangerous and should be restricted for the sake of our poor children, who will inherit the debt.

If the mint would pay off that debt and would finance the budget deficits, this might help to stop this kind of unproductive thinking. People may realize that the only limitations budget deficits of the federal government have are their possible impact on inflation. As long as the price index remains stable, the deficits are not harmful but helpful, as they make it unnecessary to expand inflationary bank credit.

People may realize that growing budget deficits of the federal government are natural phenomena for a prosperous country. Since the mint has wiped out the accumulated "debt," there is no reason anymore to gripe about the terrible burden of debt.

Please understand that this reasoning is by no means an endorsement of a growing role of the federal government. What the proper size of the government is should be discussed and fought over all the time. I am not a libertarian. I think a strong and efficient government is needed. But waste is always a problem and must be addressed all the time. The government should not try to resolve problems which people can resolve themselves without creating huge bureaucracies. For example, I favor replacing Medicare and Medicaid and private health insurance by issuing a "health card" sponsored by the federal government. This card would work mostly like a regular credit card for health-related expenses. People would be responsible for their health expenses. Only in catastrophic cases the federal government may cover the costs.

I mention this only to avoid the misconception that by advocating the empowerment of the mint I am pleading for more socialism and more government. The real issue is this: what is the best way to finance a given level of expenses? I am arguing that the burden of these expenses is lighter if they can be financed by contributions by the mint instead of by taxation.

The bigger the mint's share of the money raised to fund the government's expenses, the better off we are. Of course, this does not mean that the resources of the mint are limitless. The limits are imposed by the dangers of inflation. It is up to the policymakers to find the right mix of taxes and contributions of the mint, of additional credit and additional income in order to place the economy on a path of price stability and full employment.

This path can only be found if the income policy encourages people to work, to invest, to invent, and provide services to their fellow human beings. Of course, expenses for the unlucky, the downtrodden, the sick, and the handicapped should be part of the right mixture. But the main thrust of the policies should be to reward people's efforts. If somebody builds a new mousetrap and gets incredibly rich, that's great, and generous as Americans are, they will not envy the fellow but admire him for his smarts and his good luck. Next time around, it could be me or you who will find the road to riches.

Since the mint has the power to eliminate debt and to provide income, the question must arise as to whether the mint can spread the good stuff to the fifty state governments.

The answer is an unequivocal "no," tempered with a reluctant "maybe." Only a sovereign government has the power to produce money. Since the fifty states which form the United States have relinquished the right to issue money, only the federal government has the power to do so. The state governments must balance their budgets, as required by the constitution of most of the states. This doesn't keep many states from spending more than what they take in as tax receipts. The shortfall must be financed by issuing bonds. So once again we have a situation where governments depend on banks and capital markets. If the debt of a state grows too much, the credit-worthiness of its bonds suffers and interest rates go up. Supposedly the threat of higher financing costs has a disciplinary effect on the spending habits of state governments. Nevertheless, many states—as some municipalities—have amassed huge debt loads. In some cases, it appears that bankruptcy is a possibility.

Although this system may not be perfect, I see no viable alternative to it. Only this way a currency block with a multitude of member states, like the United States, can function. The member states should balance their budget and leave it to federal governments and its mint to provide the proper stimulus for the whole union. Of course, the mint can decide to channel some money as transfers to the budgets of the member states. This must be done in an equitable way. Whether this is a good way for the mint to direct a flow of incomes into the economy is disputable. Since each state government has its own priorities for spending, the effects of such income policy of the mint is hard to calculate.

These considerations can be applied as well to a looser union like Euroland, which consist of the European nations which have adopted the euro as their currency. The economies of these countries are subject to a uniform credit policy determined by the European central bank in Frankfurt. All nations conduct their fiscal policies independently. In this regard, Euroland is in some ways similar to the United States. But the difference is that in Euroland, there is no strong central state in existence. Therefore, the fiscal policies of each individual member states of Euroland have a much bigger impact on the general economic conditions than the fiscal policies of each member state of the American union.

In Euroland too, member states must finance their debt by raising money at the capital markets. It remains to be seen whether this dependence on bankers and capital investors instills the politicians in all member countries with the prudence necessary to keep the union in the proper balance.

It is certainly a possibility that some member states, which used to solve many of their problems by devaluating their currencies, could run up their debt to an extent that capital markets would demand exorbitant interest rates, which these countries can't afford. The specter of a member country going bankrupt cannot be ruled out. Imagine Italy going broke. Its debt is held by many European banks. If Italy would go bankrupt, these banks would be hurt severely, if not fatally.

Such a nightmare was haunting the German government, which tried to delay the launching of the euro until some safeguards were installed. But the French leaders suspected that Germany was dragging its feet because the population didn't want to give up the D-mark, which had served them so well. Letting the D-mark go was the price the French demanded for allowing the reunification of Germany. The German government managed, though, to put one safeguard into the fragile edifice of the euro. In the Belgian town of Maastricht, a clause was introduced which mandated that each country's budget deficit may not exceed the limit of 3 percent of its national product.

It is not without irony that Germany was the first country which could not meet these requirements. Because of the huge costs of propping up the sick economy of the former-communist-ruled Eastern provinces, running a large budget deficit would have been the right decision. What the united Germany needed was a surge of demand, a surge of production which would spread incomes all over the country. This happened for one year. The Y-component grew rapidly while inflation receded. This is another proof that budget deficits can be very beneficial to the people. Unfortunately, then-chancellor Kohl gave in to the pressure from all sides to rein in the budget deficit. A surcharge on income taxes was imposed. Immediately, the optimistic outlook was gone. The big unions demanded pay raises. Inflation re-emerged. The boom was killed, but Germany was making headway in meeting the 3 percent rule of Maastricht.

The following decade was a period of lackluster growth. The reunification became a burden to the western Germans. If the government would have kept the taxes at their prior level, the boom would have made everything easier and, ultimately, would have created plenty of savings and plenty of tax receipts.

But since the German government had insisted on setting up the 3 percent Maastricht rule, it could not disregard it without undermining it and losing credibility.

Also, most Germans are fiscals to the core. This may have something to do with the experience of the super inflation after the First World War, which wiped out their savings.

Relying on their common sense, people think that the government's spending was to blame. In reality, this inflation was the result of a gigantic credit explosion which provided fuel to the growing energy costs due to shortages because of the coal strike in response to the French occupation of the Ruhr valley.

But myths are more powerful than reality, especially when they fit into preconceptions of the people who have an unshakable belief in their common sense. And their common

sense tells them, inflation is always proof, that the government
lives beyond its means. Sacrifices are called for, aren't they?
"*Meister Masoch* is always popular," the economist Helmut
Arndt liked to say. But we have shown that the most entrenched
sort of inflation is the cyclical inflation, which is due to a lack
of income-financed demand and too much credit-financed
demand.

By their fixation on the limits of budget deficits, the
founders of the euro have reduced the chances that the
European currency can survive the turmoil to be expected at
the end of the disinflationary upswing. There are plenty of
highly respected economic thinkers who are predicting the
demise of the euro. Most of them argue that the lacking central
fiscal policy will doom the European currency.

While I acknowledge that some of the member countries
may run the risk of bankruptcy which could endanger all of
Euroland, the politicians and the general public should be
reminded that the bigger danger for the euro lies in a surge
of credit-financed demand and lagging income-financed
demand.

True, Euroland needs a solid fiscal policy by its member
states, a determined struggle against waste and corruption,
and measures to streamline bloated governments.

On the other hand, Euroland needs more income-financed
demand, which makes it possible to restrict credit-financed
demand.

Both requirements seem to contradict each other. But they
are not. Both can be realized with a European mint.

I envision a system which mandates either a balanced budget or some deficit limitations, like the Maastricht 3 percent rule. At the same time the mint should offer each compliant member state a transfer of money, boosting the income of each of its citizens if the prevailing economic conditions permit such largess. Preferably, the states with trade surpluses should receive more money per person than the states with trade deficits.

Furthermore, the mint should reward all states which stick to the budget rules with a sizable reduction of its accumulated debt. A good start would be to wipe out all debt in the amount of 20 percent of each state's national product. Later on the debt load could be reduced further.

Eliminating all public debt is not my first priority since I consider the bond market a good avenue for the retirement of money. The retirement of money is the other condition for establishing a monetary system of mint money, which allows inflation to remain at zero percent. But wiping out all public debt can be done. In that case, the reserve requirements of banks must be tightened. Some people may buy gold, silver, and other precious metals. I am not against that, because holding gold is another way of retiring money and taking it out of circulation. This provides the mint the opportunity to create new money which can be channeled to its most productive use. Gold prices may go through the roof. But remember, the gold bubble may burst, which may convince more people that saving mint money is the safest investment.

Don't believe the bankers who predict a surge of inflation if the mint wipes out government "debt." Not true! Most of the public debt is financed by central bank credit, which will just evaporate. Everybody is better off, besides the people who until then could produce money "out of thin air" in order to provide credit for their speculation.

I am convinced that the big crisis at the end of the third phase of the long waves will rock the euro. Some euro countries, which prospered because the European central bank conducts a uniform credit policy allowing real estate prices to soar, will experience a huge contraction when the bubble bursts, resulting in a surge of their budget deficits. The task at hand will be to strengthen the demand for goods and services of the Y-component without letting the growing deficits create turmoil at the capital markets. I don't know how this can be done with central bank money. But I know that mint money can overcome the contradictions inherent in the system of money created by credit. An empowered mint can steer the economy from the brink of the depression to an era of solid growth, zero inflation, and high employment.

It is very unlikely, though, that such a reform of the monetary system will take place soon. So far, it seems that I am the only one who calls for such a fundamental change of the monetary system. Lacking a big-enough platform, my arguments have not found a hearing. The mainstream media is not receptive. Knowing how journalism works, I gave up on journalists. Most of them can't grasp anyhow what I am talking about.

Most media types are opportunists anyway, and of course, (without knowing it) they believe in the mythos of the *Klapperstorch*, which drops the newborn money out of the thin air on the banks. It's a powerful mythos and a taboo which can only be questioned by people of strong character and deep convictions. They exist, I am sure. I am embarking on a grassroots campaign to find them. I am confident the time will come when these people will decide that it is highly important to put banks in their proper place—and empower the mint.

Chapter 10
People, Hear the Signals!

When the big crisis is coming, the socialists of various persuasions will feel vindicated in their staunch disapproval of the capitalist economic order. The idea that socialism is the salvation may not inspire the majority of Americans, but it remains a potent dream of intellectuals who are disgusted by the frivolous consumer society. But even people who cherish economic freedom may now ask themselves whether capitalism isn't fundamentally flawed.

I can only hope that when the critical stage arrives, the politicians will have gained some understanding about the true nature of money and its impact on the economy. I hope people will understand by then that the malaise is not the consequence of the market economy but the result of the current monetary system. Like the *Socialiste Internationale*, I admonish the people to hear the signals—but the right signals, please!

Socialism and a planned economy are not the right answer to the crisis. Needed is "only" a fundamental change of the monetary system. To steer the country in the right direction to such a reform would be difficult enough and has only a chance if there are enough lawmakers who are not corrupted by the vast monetary power of the banks. Such reform would encounter the resistance of the whole financial sector. After all, who wants to give up the power to rule the world? The most ardent supporters of the banks would be the speculators who amassed gigantic fortunes during the last decade.

At this point in time (1990), we probably only went through half of the disinflationary upswing during the third phase of the long waves. It is most likely that the speed and the scope of the speculation will increase further until the last crescendo ends.

The following collapse of the economy could be even more pronounced than during the Depression in the thirties because the current disinflationary upswing will be much longer than the third phase of the long waves ending with the crash of 1929. That disinflationary upswing lasted only a decade because the peak of the inflation after the end of World War I was less than half a high as the one in 1980. The higher the peak of inflation, the longer is the slope to the bottom. Therefore, the current disinflationary upswing has roughly ten years more to go and may become wobbly around the turn of the century.

The wealth which will have been created until then will surpass anything which the world has seen so far. Already now, the class of the nouveau riche is setting the social climate. In New York City, where I live, the new order is very much on display. Wealth can be a good thing, especially when the wealthy have gained their fortunes by honest achievements to the benefit to their fellow human beings. Much of the new wealth doesn't have this quality and therefore arouses envy. The new wealth stinks.

It would be good if the fortunes made by speculation would vanish by speculation as well. It can be argued that the crash of the stock market and the collapse of the real estate market and the following depression would help to restore the proper balance. But unfortunately such a crisis would hurt the working population much more than the rich speculators. A depression must be avoided, even if the countervailing measures do not only benefit the so-called little guys, but Dagobert Duck and his peers swimming in money.

But at least the empowerment of the mint would provide means to policymakers to make the distribution of incomes more even, to stabilize the level of employment, and eradicate inflation permanently. mint money can be directed to those who need it and who would spend most of it to meet their living expenses. The increased demand creates the conditions for capital investments, which increase the supply of goods. In a functioning, competitive market economy, more demand creates more supplies and the production of more supplies creates more demand.

It is true, the heaps of monies accumulated during the third phase of the long waves wouldn't disappear, and by stabilizing the Y-component of the economy, the slide of the stock and real estate prices would be halted.

But policymakers now have the opportunity to establish a sound basis to the economy. It is their task to select the right dosage of newly created money and to choose the best path of it into the economy. The empowerment of the mint provides the opportunity to give paper money the characteristics of gold money, as part of it is introduced into the economy as income and, as savings, is retired.

Now we have the pleasure of talking about the good news, which comes with a drop of inflation to zero percent when the mint is in charge of regulating the money supply. As long as the central bank has this responsibility, there is only one way to escape from deflation and depression: by cranking up the credit machine. This may work. Inflation may become the savior for a while. But only if the central bank feeds the monster more and lets it grow. As soon as the central bankers try to moderate the inflation, the economy is back on the road to the abyss of the depression.

Cyclical inflation is the result of too little income-financed demand for parts of the Y-component and too much credit-financed demand for parts of the X-component.

I know this observation of mine is hard to swallow for most people, because it contradicts common sense and human intuition. When my four-legged companion Felix took me to his walks through New York's Central Park, I bothered many other dogs and their servants with sermons about the long waves and the misdirection of money caused by the banks. Most of my involuntary listeners found my reasoning quite logical and convincing. Only when I tried to explain the concept of cyclical inflation could they not follow me. The people I talked to were mostly highly intelligent, successful people. Their reaction gave me a hint of how much resistance I was likely to encounter with my general theory of long-term economic development.

There is another crucial part of my theory that the dog walkers of Central Park didn't fully understand either or considered as unrealistic. I mean the concept of "true saving" by the retirement of money.

As you know by now, I am pleading for a simulation of gold-money by paper money. I want paper money to "behave" like gold-money.

Gold is found by miners and turned into money by minters. For their service they receive incomes. Thus, the created gold-money enters the economy in the form of incomes. It sets in motion a Keynesian chain of spending and saving, which creates the national product. This process ends after all newly created gold coins have been retired. Another batch of new gold-money keeps the economy going. Here lies the secret of the stability of gold-money. minted money (paper money produced by the mint) assumes the characteristics of gold money if its production creates incomes and if the money is retired after its path through the economy. minted money does not provide incomes only to Miners, but also to the whole population to whom the mint distributes part of its profit.

Now the question remains on how the money can be retired after it took its course through the economy. The answer is this: by preventing banks from automatically using this money for issuing credit. One solution would be if savers would no longer put their savings in bank accounts but hide it under their mattress or put it into a vault. But of course, I don't want to encourage anybody to hide a collection of money bills in their home. This is much too risky. The fear of being robbed is one of the main reasons why people chose to entrust it to the banks in the first place. Bank accounts remain good places for the storage of money even if the purpose becomes its retirement. The money saved on bank accounts is retired if the banks are forced to increase their reserves.

A safer way to retire money would be to buy financial instruments issued by the mint. I propose that at all post offices people can deposit money in mint accounts. The interest paid for the deposits would be zero (as long as there is no inflation). But the savers can be absolutely sure that their savings would not be used for risky speculations and would not disappear when a bank collapses.

It is not so that the government depends on the funds saved by the population in order to finance budget deficits. The mint can take care of that problem. The bonds issued may have the legal form of debt. But in the economic sense, they constitute no debt but true savings, retired money.

When inflation drops to zero percent and when price stability is expected in the future, the saver has to be content with a yield of zero.

The level of interest rates is the sum of three components: the scarcity of money, the compensation for inflation, and the reward for taking risks. There is no scarcity of money and no inflation when the mint steers the economy in the right direction. Therefore, people can only expect a return on their savings if they let the bank use it for providing credit. Actually, according to my interpretation, those funds are not saved but invested, and because they share the risks attached to their usage by the bank, they must garner some interest. On the other hand, retired savings do not fetch interest because they constitute money, not debt.

This may sound like a bad deal for the savers. But don't forget that true savers can sleep much better than investors because their money is safe and keeps its value.

The most secure form of true saving would be if we humans would follow the example of the dormouse and would accumulate enough hazelnuts and other vital products to survive the winter of our life. Unfortunately, our refrigerators and storage facilities do not have enough capacity for this form of real, true saving. Also, the national product is like a cake, which must be baked fresh all the time.

How can humans under these circumstances protect themselves against future shortages of hazelnuts and losses of income? The hoarding of gold coins or mint money is, so to speak, a simulation of the hoarding of hazelnuts. It's a pity that neither gold nor mint money can be eaten in the case of need. The savers must exchange the gold coins or mint money against items which can be eaten and sustain the livelihood. The uncompromising upkeep of price stability is therefore the pivot of the mint money system.

Saving gold or mint money is individual saving, not collective saving. The saved money is an overhang to the national product. It is not covered by any other assets. In a system of central bank money, this is different. Here all saved money is covered by assets. After all, according to Keynes, I = S, savings equal investment. When money is created by the central bank, the dormouse doesn't collect nuts anymore; it finances the production facilities which allow future increases in the output of hazelnuts.

The system of central bank money according to the interpretation of Keynes and most mainstream economists seems to be logical. But in fact, it isn't, because savings does not equal capital investments automatically.

I = S is only correct if S is defined as savings used for investment, which turns the equation in a tautology, a truism like one apple equals one apple.

The truth is that after the first phase of the long waves has ended, savings exceed capital investment and the banks use the excess of saving funds for other profitable purposes, like financing the price increases of commodities and real estate—and feeding inflation.

In a monetary system based on gold coins or minted money, investments do not have to absorb all savings, because the saved money is retired. The gap of demand because of the retirement of these monies is filled by the production of new money, which creates streams of incomes and spending, helping to utilize and expand production capacities. mint money resembles the system which the airlines use to fill all the seats of their airplanes. They issue more tickets than the available number of each airplane because they know that a certain percentage of bookings always will be canceled due to the changed personal circumstances of the travelers. The overhang of tickets allows airlines to make good use of the seating capacities of their planes. This ticket overhang dissolves as soon as the planes are in the air. That is not the case with the minted money as it is retired, often for many years. The minted money has the tendency to accumulate—very much like the gold used to pile up in the American homes until 1933 when, by a presidential executive order, the private ownership of gold was forbidden and all the private holding had to be sold to the U.S. government. The gold stored in Fort Knox is a monetary overhang, meaning that this money is not covered by any other assets. The gold owned by the government constitutes collective savings only insofar as the U.S. nation now has reserves of a metal, which other nations in an emergency would accept as means of payment.

While saved mint money in all other regards is useless as a means of collective saving of the U.S. nation, it can serve as reserves of all other nations, very much like the dollars created by the central bank. The difference is, though, that mint money can keep its value much better than central bank money. mint money can sustain existing world trade patterns better than central bank money, which tends to lose in value and therefore is not such a good medium for the collective savings of other nations.

Nations which "manage" their exchange rates and enjoy trade surpluses amass such dollar reserves, not by choice but out of necessity. These nations are keeping their dollar holdings in U.S. bank accounts, thus providing those banks with more money to be recycled via issuing credit. The trade surplus of other nations like Germany, which don't manipulate the exchange rate of their currency, may pile up some dollar reserves in the bank accounts of their export firms, but the mechanism of the currency markets tends to limit the size of such reserves.

Especially smaller countries are better off when they own such reserves. They tend to buffer these countries against currency swings. But the huge trade surpluses of countries like Japan, Taiwan, and Germany are signs that their monetary and fiscal policies are counterproductive. The harmful effects on the world economy which these surpluses have can be reduced if the accumulated dollar surpluses are retired and not recycled. If these countries use the money to "invest" in stocks or in commodities. they tend to feed inflation. Luckily, mint money keeps its value if the mint finds the proper dosage and the proper avenue for its newly produced money. So here again we are dealing with the problem of restraining the recycling of money by the banks in order to channel funds to a more productive use.

The trade surpluses of some nations mean trade deficits for others. Especially the huge trade deficits of the United States are often looked upon as a sign of American weakness and lacking competitiveness. But it can be looked at as a sign of American strength as well.

In a famously misleading commentary with the headline THE TWIN TOWERS OF THE BUDGET DEFICIT AND THE TRADE DEFICIT, the *New York Times* reinforced the common sense wisdom that budget deficits and trade deficits have the same roots. But these twin towers were not built with the same stuff. The only causal relationship is that an economy which grows faster than others due to the stimulating effect of budget deficits tends to import more than it exports. Therefore, trade deficits can be a sign of economic strength rather than weakness. Nations other than the USA could not endure with chronic trade deficits. Only the United States can live with trade deficits of such magnitude, because of the status of the dollar as reserve currency. The other nations depending on their exports should be grateful for this unique role of the dollar.

Often the question is asked how long the United States can afford to borrow money in order to finance their budget deficits. Of course, this question is based on confused thinking because the United States does not need to borrow from other nations to finance its budget deficit. It can produce its own money, thank you. It is not true either that trade deficits require borrowing. American importers pay their bills with dollars, with internationally accepted money, that is. If Americans buy Toyotas, they get the cars and the Japanese get the dollars. Transaction closed.

It's up to the Japanese what to do with those dollars. It makes total sense for them to accumulate these dollars. In ten years they are probably worth more than the Toyotas, which may begin to rust.

It is not true either that America depends on the Japanese being nice and using their surplus of dollars for the purchase of U.S. bonds. Actually, the Japanese could bury their dollars into the sands of the desert Gobi. That would be a satisfactory solution for the Americans because this way the dollars would be retired. But it would not hurt either if the surplus nations

-172- Jes Rau

would buy treasuries with these funds. Not that the American need these funds. But for the Japanese, these bonds would be the perfect storage devices of value—as long as the mint is able to keep the price level stable. Remember, economically speaking, U.S. bonds are not debts but true saving.

Therefore, mint money makes it possible to keep the current order of the world economy intact. Under these circumstances there are no set limits for U.S. trade deficits as long as the surplus Dollars are retired.

This is by no means an endorsement for persisting U.S. trade deficits. The excessive imports weaken the industrial base of America, they weaken the Y-component, they diminish income-financed demand, and that encourages the banks to lend more money for speculative purposes. In America, political decisions are usually made to satisfy the rich. Politicians can be bought easily by contributions to their reelection campaigns. If parasites become big enough, they take over the whole organism. This is certainly true also for societies.

America turns more and more into a banana republic governed by a small "elite," if you want to bestow that expression to the people who misuse their exclusive role in a systematic fashion.

The forces which may try to reverse the trend currently are much too weak to overcome the power of the financial sector and of big businesses. In order to restrain the banks, fundamental changes must take place, which can only be accomplished if a groundswell of public opinion is changing the whole political landscape. I have serious doubt that the nature of the U.S. Congress and of the U.S. government can be changed within the existing system. I think a parliamentary democracy modeled after the European one would be much preferable to the current form of electing Congress and the president. This, of course, is just a dream. So we have to work within the existing system and try our best to get people who think about the common good first instead about their own gain of power and riches elected.

The big U.S. companies must be pressured as well to take into account the effects of their actions on the American people. All big industrial companies have production facilities in foreign countries. They can still make money even if the trade deficit worsens and the industrial base of this country shrinks further. They can even make money if Americans would go down the drain.

Of course, cheap imports have tremendous benefits to the public as well. They help keep the price level downs which in turn enlarges the wiggle room for monetary expansion. If the central bank is in charge, credit-financed demand grows further, encouraging speculation. If the mint has been empowered, income-financed demand can be expanded, which could offset some of the damage done to the Y-component by the surge of imports.

Another danger for the reserve status of the dollar could come from the euro. Many countries with large dollar reserves could be tempted to exchange some of their holdings of the American currency into euros. Some Europeans already boast that the euro might more and more replace the dollar as a reserve currency. But Europeans have no reason to gloat. To shoot for the status of a reserve currency wouldn't contribute much to the health of the European economy. The exchange rate of the euro versus the dollar would rise, and Europe would have to absorb a flood of imports. I doubt whether their industries would be happy about that.

Europeans would fool themselves if they would interpret the current rise of the euro's exchange rate as proof of its underlying strength. The forces which shape the currency market rarely have something do with that "invisible hand" which supposedly regulates all markets efficiently. The currency market is the playground of speculators with almost unlimited deep pockets. After all, the banks can provide all the credit they want for that purpose.

The rising exchange rate of the euro is by no means proof that the euro has established itself as a viable currency in the long run. As long as member states of Euroland are forced to finance their budget deficits by loans, each country can become subject to massive speculation, which raises the cost of these loans and might even drive them into bankruptcy.

I would be much more optimistic about the future of the euro if their member countries would turn it into a currency which behaves like a gold-currency, as new money is injected into the economy as income and retired when it has run its course through the economy. A European mint could conduct the policies necessary to establish permanent price stability.

The system of minted money, like the system of gold-money, is based on the trust of the citizens in the enduring value of the currency. This trust must be earned by policymakers by conducting a monetary policy which includes elements of fiscal policy affecting not only the rates for bank credit, but also the net income of all people. The system of mint money is rooted in the economic freedom of the people. The government, as the owner of the mint, has the responsibility to create the proper amount of money and to distribute it in a way which makes everybody profit from it. It is up to the individual citizen how he or she spends the money. I call that true democracy. I call that market economy for everybody.

Of course, the mint could use part of the newly produced money to fund infrastructure improvements and other projects. But I favor the disbursement to individuals in the form of tax cuts and contributions to Social Security. The funding for other projects should be done by the regular budget process.

But the mint should not be involved only in income policies. It should intervene on the credit side as well by refinancing mortgages and by lightening the burden of credit card debt. The banks are of course not eager to do these themselves. Actually, the banks cannot play a constructive role when the third phase of the long waves comes to an end.

The power of the banks must be reduced sharply, at least temporarily until the economy moves on an even keel. But the banks would still play a crucial role. It remains their responsibility to provide credit to investors who make the economy grow. The banks may continue to get part of their funding from the central bank. But the central bank no longer fetches that money out of thin air. The stork may still bring the babies, but not the newborn money anymore. The central bank has to get the money the old-fashioned way. It has to borrow it from the mint.

The banks will still be powerful. But the power to create new money they will have to cede to the mint.

It may even sound ludicrous to talk about such a change in the role of banks at a time when we are experiencing a boom which seems to be endless and which enriches so many people who have access to almost unlimited bank credit. But believe me, the power of the long waves is unbroken.

I do not claim to be a prophet who can determine the exact date when all the trouble begins. Of course, I do not know either whether policymakers will take some measures affecting the length and the shape of the long waves. Who knows, perhaps they will decide to cut some taxes. And perhaps the central bank will make a U-turn in its credit policy. But assuming that the politicians do not change the current course of the economy, my estimate is that the third phase of the long wave now (1990) has gone through half of its length. I think that the third phase will roughly stretch over twenty years, like both preceding phases. (The first phase of expansion took place in the forties and fifties. The second phase of the inflationary upswing started in the beginning of the sixties and ended at the last year of the seventies.)

The third phase of the disinflationary upswing started at the beginning of the eighties and may end at the last year of the nineties. Well, 2000 is a nice round number. I think the year 2000 could prove to be a significant turning point in the development of the American economy and the world economy. This could be the year when we reach the point where the dangers of a beginning depression become apparent. Of course, it could be earlier, and it could be a few years later. But I think the year 2000 is the landmark which we should use for our planning. Now the time has come to prepare for taking countermeasures. Now the time has come to listen to the following hymn:

Peoples, hear the signals (but the right ones)!
The time has come to stop the depression.
The time has come to eradicate inflation.
The time has come to abolish unemployment.
The time has come for more justice.

Peoples, hear the signals (but the right ones)!
The time has come to shake off the yoke of the banks.
The time has come to abolish central bank money.
The time has come to introduce money, which is as good as gold.
The time has come to retire the savings.
The time has come to empower the mint.
Peoples, hear the signals (but the right ones)!